ICE COLD MURDER

AUTHOR
Michael A Chambers

Copyright - Michael Andrew Chambers

Publishing history – 1st Edition

Printed by CMP Digital Print Solutions – Dorset

ISBN 978-0-9539398-3-1

Published by M. A. Chambers

Special thanks to:

The girlfriend - Ligaya, who has helped me on the computer and putting up with all the moaning!

The first proof reader Emma Dilley who helped on the two opening introductions

And as regards the front cover.....Paul Breeze

CONTENTS

Acknowledgements

Introduction

Foreword

The Town Of Merrivale
Key to map
Town map
Street map

The Season

ACKNOWLEDGEMENTS

To all the characters in this book who are real people – though the storyline fictitious. So, fans, officials and ex-players and foe of the Nottingham Panthers Ice hockey team who didn't mind me using their names plus the Sheffield Blazers recreational Ice Hockey team for photos. Grateful thanks.

Paul Breeze

The second and main proof reader - Paul Breeze - for the time taken to check the story in between his own hockey duties.

Steve Flemming for the foreword

Plus those who joined in with this venture

MERRIVALE MODEL VILLAGE in Gt.Yarmouth
For their permission to use photographic material and name

Mary's Café…The Legends Bar and Bunkers Hill Bar
For advertisement and name inclusions to the story

Plus Mansfield photo venues - Ten-pin Bowling, Festival Hall and Manor Squash club – and Mrs Maureen Smyth for photo scenes

Introduction and Special Notes

After a computer self published hardback of my family's involvement in hockey (a pictorial) I ventured into two ISBN published books on the Nottingham Panthers Ice Hockey team followed by one for the UK governing body regards the Great Britain national side.

My interest of creating these 'pieces' have been mainly of factual and statistical content, with some literal work to compliment it.
Then I thought I'd branch out on a new venture of a short story centered on my love of the sport.

Not being so hot on the written word I had to ask for help in checking the work and thanks again to all who have given their time for free, as this is again a small non-profit making composition. Of specialised theme for the hockey market, which is a limited edition book? But if you do eventually find it among the Oscar nominations on TV as a possible award winning film you'll know I had finally made it with the rights to its storyline being bought for the big screen. I wish....

Conceived from someone else's idea to use a few 'real' people as characters (the book 'Second Destiny' by Steve M. Smith) I asked people from the independent hockey forum 'The Cage' if they'd like to be involved, then proceeded to ask a few other officials and ex-players whom I have passed by in my 37 odd years following the game.

Then firms and establishments of note also involved in hockey were asked for their permission to pen them into the books story as well as sponsor this venture.

One such person in this book is a fellow Black and Gold member of the crowd who left our ranks when she passed away during this work being put together. Her daughter, who is also a supporter, immediately stated that she wanted mum to still be included within the pages (whatever character) as mum had asked to be in it from the start. So this is also a big thank you from me to ALL the fans that have moved on to that big arena in the sky having given their following to our teams over the years. We salute these people, the life blood of clubs all around the countries in our league. **Sandi Stephenson**, I hope you had a great time whether they were low or high emotions.

****

I think I have two more books left in me. A historical account of the sport with all the winners listed, perhaps a small pocket book to keep all our memories in.

The second may be a book to encourage and inform the younger of our fans to understand and perhaps get involved more in the sport and the book to be a possible resource of information of how to go about it?

Another might be a compilation of the Nottingham Panthers to update the previous books. Now then, that's three and I'm getting ahead of myself so let's just see.

After THAT big film deal I'll be back on this beach. But until then thank you for the purchase of this book.

To Ligaya (Ging)...Xx

Advertisement

With many other attractions and its own Tea room and gift shop

A leisurely stroll around the railway and gardens is for all ages

Found on the seafront of Great Yarmouth on Norfolk's East coast
—

Marine Parade, Great Yarmouth, Norfolk, NR30 3JG
01493 842097

www.merrivalemodelvillage.co.uk

FOREWORD

Written by Steve Flemming

Anyone who knows Mick Chambers will be aware that his middle name is 'statistics', you could seriously fill a small library with his memorabilia collection alone.

Facts and figures are not everyone's cup of tea but Mick seems to embrace it with an amazing passion. This has led to him writing books, in particular relating to the Great Britain Ice Hockey Team. In addition, he has contributed to other publications and even now collects all the statistics from each and every Nottingham Panthers game.

His love affair with Ice Hockey and the Panthers goes back to the very early days. I have been fortunate to view some items in his collection; the range is incredible. He attempts to keep everything in mint condition, looking back at moments in time is just the norm for him.

It was quite thrilling to me to be able to view information dating back to 1936. This was the year that the Great Britain Ice Hockey team won the Winter Olympics, World and European Championships; this was staged in Garmisch-Partenkirchen, West Germany, fascinating information.

Actually Mick goes to great lengths in his attempts to add to his collection, always looking for that special item that might become available. It would be excellent if at some point all of these hidden gems could be available for all to view.

The latest project for Mick is to write another book, *Ice Cold Murder*. However, this is a book with a difference! To be quite honest when I started to read through some of the contents, I began to realise that Mick has some imagination.

This story is centred on a local Ice Hockey team. It sort of reminded me of Melchester Rovers, this was the fictional football team portrayed in a comic strip; Roy Race (Roy of the Rovers) was the main character.

This book though is obviously light hearted; it carries a real sense of humour, I am still having this vision of Ice Hockey night featuring Aspley and Clifton?

Despite all the funny moments that Mick creates in the book, there is a story line that leads to a darker tale of murder, a kind of mystery that plays out amongst the hockey players and arena staff.

To conclude, the book is most enjoyable, it is 'tongue-in-cheek' of course and you will soon pick up on that. This is something away from statistics, although Mick still finds a moment to include some information on his new team with the league tables.

When describing the book for marketing purposes, *Ice Cold Murder* does not fit into the usual categories, you simply have to read it and find a description for yourself.

Good luck with the publication.

Steve Flemming

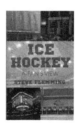

Author of *Ice Hockey 'A Fans View'*

 - *Check out steveflemming.co.uk for his blogs*

The Town Of Merrivale

Driving north wasn't difficult but Merrivale seemed to be miles from anywhere. For some time on the right you could see a string of mountains on the horizon with nothing but flat arid land between it and the road. Contrasting this, on the left, was a wooded area with marshes that crept up and almost touched the car tyres; it was not somewhere you would like to venture.

A dirt track swung left, away into this forest of green which would eventually take you to the local estate of Morgantown. It was not somewhere a person would choose to live. Housing was poor and you would have to drive back to Merrivale for your essentials as there was not much else happening that way.

Just after this turn and ahead of you was a large wooden archway over the road, with the words 'Welcome to Merrivale' spread across it. The first inhabitants could be seen here. They were two elderly gentlemen working away to make good the sign that seemed to have worn from age. Behind you, two hours driving and a lonely landscape, it was good to be approaching civilisation.

The town was very inviting and the dusty road suddenly became a street. 'Lord Percy Street' as named on a large sign when you entered the hub. Curbs were neat and well balanced with lampposts and signage a plenty. Suddenly you were in the thick of life after a bleak time stuck in what had seemed like a desert of a place for the last 120 miles.

On the right, shops, restaurants, leisure facilities and factory outlets could be seen, even a boat yard, although there wasn't much water around for miles bar a small lake behind the shops. There was even a small gauge train track which operated delivery services to the community facilities and caution was needed when this was in operation. The mêlée of business and entertainment went on as far as the eye could see. On the left, tall workplace buildings and office units, gloomy looking features but a hive of employment for many of the town's folk. These ugly brick square shaped buildings with the usual glass windows floor upon floor ran for a while, and then - as if to break the monotony between them - there were a few smaller ones.

Looking west between these buildings, you could pick out large domestic flats when a break in the structures allowed. But other than one early left turn that took you behind the office blocks, no other roads led to this estate. It was, however, accessible on foot but only through overgrown greenery laid waste - which made it difficult. You would definitely have to be a local to know your way around here, although the thoroughfares and shops opposite allowed easy passage to the much better housing and units to the east.

Still driving north, after the last towering office block on the left 'Chambers Logistics Incorporated' and a smaller one 'Atkins Limited', the oldest and biggest structure of all could be seen, set back from its boundary railings, in its own grounds . It wasn't a particularly great structure but stood proud and was a breath of fresh air after what had gone before. It wasn't leaning over you like those towering office blocks that sat on the street's edge with only the public footpath and a small slither of grass between it and the road. Here there was open space between you and the large building.

You wouldn't even know what this place stood for or what it did until you got to the main entrance which had the words 'Ice Stadium' hanging up on the gates.

A solitary notice board on the railings was the only other clue of what might have originally been guessed at as an old factory closed down many years ago. The notice board displayed skating characters and pictures of the interior as if to convey what could be enjoyed there. It was also the home of the Merrivale Mustangs Ice Hockey team. It wasn't pretty but certainly very colourful ......in blue.

The perimeter fencing continued a long way beyond the rink. A car park on the inside of the railings was adjacent to what can only be described as large industrial sized bins set before a forest of trees. The car park offering some protection to customers rather than leaving their vehicles on the main road but this was generally an empty space most of the week. It was not until you got to the end of the building that you realised it was the 'Ice Stadium' as written up on high with the town's motif emblazoned either side of the name.

Its main gates faced a pretty landscaped corner plot over the road which had Monarch Street to its left as you looked across. This ran away east from Lord Percy Street and onwards up to a coastal town called East Craig. The landscaped gardens had a cobbled pedestrian way that led to a Parisian type 'Faulkner Square', full of flamboyant shops, café's and the only inn in town that offered rooms. Many were vacant though as this wasn't really a place to visit in winter and no one had any reason to rest over. People would normally drive straight through Merrivale (less having business at the local lodge or campsite) or were one of the 125,000 mostly living in housing on this Eastern side of the main road.

Hockey fans would flock from Monarch Street behind the gardens and cut through the square in order to cross over to the stadium on match days. The gates didn't open until half an hour before face off, so fans tended to loiter here hanging about the square with other Saturday shoppers.

Monarch Street was the main road to/from Lord Percy Street unless you had passed several hundred yards more beyond the stadium. An array of diverse establishments lay nearer the top end of town. A fishing tackle shop, MOT car testing station and a few old shacks lay bare before a lone flower shop at the top end of Percy Street. This signalled a junction of sorts that gave three alternatives. Turn right and you're into Knight Avenue which led back into the major housing estate (like Monarch Street did) with hundreds of two storey homes all very similar to each other. These had some single storey convenience shops sited within or had the odd bar on street corners, council office, library or petrol station on land set aside.

Local petrol station

Otherwise you could turn left into Branford Avenue from the end of Lord Percy Street where farm or major commercial works could be seen before you'd sweep away into the wilderness again towards the town of Chandale which was the nearest large town of note and an attractive destination at that.

Finally you could have driven straight on to what is now rough ground. The road went nowhere other than behind the northerly most part of the community and it wasn't maintained at all. People had just given up on it as access was much better from Monarch Street and Knight Avenue. It was pot holed and unsafe.

Merrivale was a town split into three parts. The majority of homes set east behind the major trading places containing the lake and where the main roads of Knight Avenue and Monarch Street met as a major junction. A second and very large extension of homes lay to the north end, built as if an afterthought as the town grew. Then a smaller suburb that hid behind the office buildings on the west side, which were behind those grim towering units, less popular because of the creeping wastes of the woodland marshes from Morgantown not far off.

Leading off from Knight Avenue was the only other link road that was often used. This was favoured by people leaving Merrivale on the north east side of town, and led to Port Raven - not actually a port at all but a near coastal town. This street was aptly called 'Port Raven Way'. It was a minor road but used regularly by folk as it split through the housing estate.

On this winding stretch the Mustangs hockey team owner Mark Atkin had his main 'M A Enterprises' business empire from which Manager Tom Higson worked on Merrivale Mustangs Ice Hockey team's affairs for the club as well as many other 'Atkin' interests.

Tom would convene 'dealings' here in the morning then move onto the stadium' smaller offices - 'Atkins Limited' on Lord Percy Street – after a game, which was next to the blue building but not in the grounds, yet access could be gained via a small gate in the side railings.

He'd usually meet there with the coach after a Saturday game. Usually watching the 2nd period, then would drop back into that office to leave the takings in a small safe before driving back with the coach to Port Raven Way to end a busy day.

Lord Percy Street

Out of Town Places

Mill works just off from Brantford Avenue

Farm land before the road moves on to Chandale

Agriculture on the outskirts going north

The slate works West of Lord Percy Street

Wood mill also West of Lord Percy Street

The Merrivale Summer Caravan Club bathed in 'winter' sunshine

KEY TO MAP OF MERRIVALE

A) LORD PERCY STREET

B) 'Atkins' Limited' Office next to the Stadium.

C) ICE STADIUM with Faulkener Square opposite

D) MONARCH STREET leading to EAST CRAIG

E) BRANTFORD AVENUE leading to CHANDALE

F) KNIGHT AVENUE goes past Port Raven Way to Monarch Street

G) PORT RAVEN WAY leading to PORT RAVEN

Atkins Ltd entrance looking across from Faulkener square, Chambers Logistics (out of picture) is to the left. The front door leads straight upstairs, similar to M A Enterprises on Port Raven Way. The ground floor is rented out and that door is to the side, next to the stadium boundary, where a gate gives access into the stadium grounds.

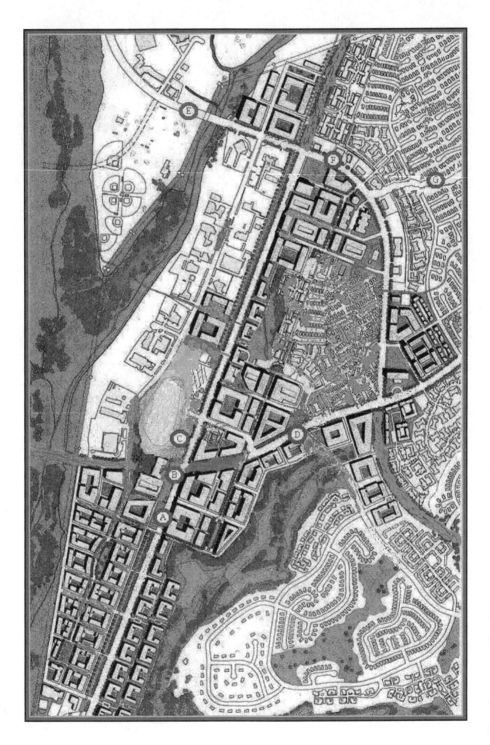

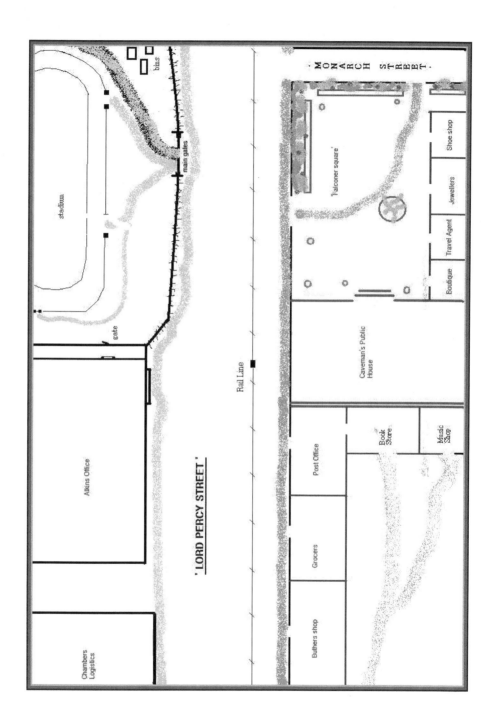

' LORD PERCY STREET '

Chambers Logistics

Atkins Office

gate

main gates

bins

stadium

Rail Line

Butchers shop

Grocers

Post Office

Book Store

Music Shop

Caveman's Public House

MONARCH STREET.

Falconer square

Boutique

Travel Agent

Jewellers

Shoe shop

The Season

It's ironic: the sport gains some recognition and becomes a popular event to attend. Thousands of fans are flocking to see their local teams but Merrivale owner Mark Atkin was none too pleased with things for his club – financially, when Ice Hockey was on the up the Mustangs were losing ground on other teams in the new National League. Where were their fans?

Things were not good and Manager, Tom Higson had a lot on his plate to turn things around. Apart from having to get the club going in the right direction, he was not a popular man. He did things his own way and there was no mediation with any of his employees, either playing, coaching or general game staff. He was trying his best but the requests he made annoyed everyone most of the time. Working hours had been cut; wages frozen after a promise of a rise and even this went no way to clearing the bills that were dropping through the letter box.

The season had started out ok with the usual press hype and marketing ploys. Yet the attendance figures were suffering and, of all things, a technical bug had hit hard, with out dated machinery breaking down on match nights. If it wasn't the zamboni one week, it was a lights failure the next and Tom was leaning on everyone to "get it right" before he'd start firing people - or at least that's what he said.

Hockey's governing body were struggling to commercialise the sport, changing formats part season or having to juggle fixtures - infuriating to say the least for fans. But luckily, along came a big concern mid 2020 that changed things overnight. Multi-millionaire tycoons offered to put money into the sport but demanded certain criteria or they'd walk away. Even with only a basic sum of money handed to club owners just now, a large proportion of the deal was due by seasons end. It was obviously too good to turn down.

With a poor bank balance and apathy from the public, hockey owners accepted the new sponsorship/management consortium, so the all new 2020/21 League, Coupe/Davis Cups and Play-Off were born. Competitions were worth winning, with prize money up for grabs; as opposed to previous ad-hoc money making affairs that congested the fixture list.

In September, Merrivale played in the first round for the 'Coupe cup' but had, as fate would have it, a poor start, losing to Aspley. Next was the start of the league campaign in October and, although games were running well, one-goal losses each match made a big dent in the points haul. Only the top ten made the play offs so people were getting a bit fractious about the season already as Merrivale were sitting a lowly 16th in the league of twenty teams.

Maybe, if Higson had the flair to get everyone on board and steer this wayward ship on course, the mid season 'Davis 'handicap' cup' tournament might see some light at the end of the tunnel. Teams that had finished poorly last season were given point's advantage in the early rounds akin to golf's handicap system so the whole set up had an evening out factor for this competition. Merrivale were drawn against top flight Carlton Scorpions, who were a shadow of their former selves - thank goodness!

Considering how the previous games had gone, the town of Merrivale were hopeful of a quarter final slot if they could just put aside Clifton Oilers (injury hit) and Toton Rangers (several bans in place) and grab that second spot in this mini league for the last eight berths in a knock out series, having beaten Bramcote twice.

On paper, the tenth placed spot in the main league from 16th was not unachievable but the team had to do better to get there. Yet the 'Daily Wind Up' newspaper journalist Mick Holland certainly thought that Merrivale might as well give up hope right now.

"The Mustangs are becoming a laughing stock of the league. On par with other clubs, we have little to offer visiting fans. Owner Mr Atkins stringent time schedules and operating guidelines leave fans queuing outside in cold temperatures waiting to gain entry to an unwelcoming stadium that needs some décor improvement. Where has all this splash of money gone that was handed out by the new league owners? Certainly not into the product offered to fans. The experience on a match night, added to what seems like a formality one goal loss every game, adds up to a failed season already. What hope for the future if the club state that there is little money in the pot?"

+ + + + + + + +

It's Saturday, game day. Carlton Scorpions are in town.
Win this and get some points from Clifton and Toton for a quarter-final place.
The team list has gone up on the outside perimeter railings and the club motto
'Respect all – fear none' is blazoned on the headed paper underneath it was the rota of players.

Davis Handicap Cup January 23rd 2021

Goal	# 94	Neil Edwards
Goal	# 01	Frankie Killen
Defence	# 02	Graham Waghorn
Defence	# 03	Steve Butler (Assistant Captain)
Defence	# 29	Wayne Pitchford
Defence	# 36	Paul Hacking
Defence	# 04	Tom Norton
Forward	# 10	Bob Marshall
Forward	# 23	Andy Barton
Forward	# 29	Adi Collins
Forward	# 05	Angel Nikolov
Forward	# 06	Johan Molin
Forward	# 07	Steve Pelletier
Forward	#08	Daniel Scott
Forward	# 09	Shaun Yardley
Forward	# 11	Rhys McWilliams
Forward	# 12	Gary Stefan (Captain)
Forward		Will Weldon (tbc)

'Respect all – fear none'

Letter to all Club Managers- at start of season

This coming season will see Two Cups, a Domestic League and the Play Off's in 2020-21.

To avoid 'double up' games and create more competition the new season will have the Coupe Knock-out Cup played first then a league schedule starts, a handicap Davis Cup competition begins mid season with finally the Play-Offs as described in the attached diagram. (See next two pages).

Some teams will play more games than others due to tournament success but competitions have been adjusted to give all clubs as equal a quantity of games per season as possible.

Coupe Cup format

Teams drawn will play two legged home and away games (bar round 1) to a quarter and semi two legged match before a final 'three game' series. The first round of games will have eight sides play for the right to join the already waiting twelve that had a 'bye' to a sixteen team round two.

League and Play Off

The usual once home and away format completes a finalised 38 game schedule from which the top ten will qualify to the play offs competition.

League places seventh to tenth will be grouped together to meet each other in round robin play. This is stage one where only the top 2 qualify.

At stage two, places one to four play each other in group A. The top two move to the semi-final and losers to stage three. Fifth and sixth league finishers will play stage one qualifier's from the 7th to 10th group in stage 2 B. The eventual two winning sides here will meet the stage two (A) losers. See attached*

Davis Handicap Cup

Four groups of five teams will play out round robin games followed by two legged knock out quarter and semi finals before a single grand final. Last season's bottom five will get a graded point's allocation as a handicap similar to the 11th to 15th placed teams getting a smaller point allocation. More details on this later.

Summary

It is a 20 team league; on a 38 game schedule AFTER an early 'Coupe K-O Cup' competition starts when a preliminary first round is followed by a 16 team round two, two legged quarter, semi and then a three game final. Mid League campaign the Davis Handicap Cup has a 20 team first round with 4 round robin groups of 5 then a 2 legged home and away quarter and semi final stage, ending in a final match too. The end of season Play-Offs then completes the season.

Merrivale Mustangs in practice session

The season thus far
_COUPE CUP
First round - 1 game (end September)

Bulwell*	5	Meadows	3
Hucknall*	3	Colwick	1
Merrivale	0	Aspley*	1
Wollaton*	6	Beeston	5

Second round - 2 legged games (end October)
(12 teams with a bye plus 4 winners from first round)

Bulcote	0-3,6-7=6-10	Gedling
Bulwell*	2-4,3-2=5-6	Aspley*
Carlton	5-2,6-2=11-4	Bestwood
Clifton	5-4,5-3=10-7	Sherwood
Hucknall*	0-8,0-2=0-10	Eastwood
Lenton	5-3,3-1=8-4	Wollaton*
Mapperley	3-0,5-1=8-1	Bramcote
Toton	3-5,5-3ot=9-8	West Bridgford

Quarter and Semi final – 2 legs played end January (draw to follow)
Final (3 legs) – played early February

****

DAVIS CUP

First round - (played January) – part complete

Group 1- 5 teams
Bestwood, Bramcote, Eastwood, Meadows, West Bridgford

Group 2 -5 teams
Bulcote, Carlton, Clifton, Merrivale, Toton

Group 3 -5 teams
Aspley, Beeston, Bulwell, Colwick, Gedling

Group 4 -5 teams
Hucknall, Lenton, Mapperley, Sherwood, Wollaton

Quarter final (2 legs) – played early March

Semi-final (2 legs) –played mid March

Final (single game) – played end March

27

Diagram to play-off schedule*

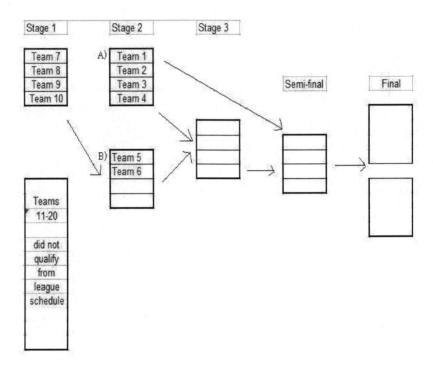

All stages of play are round robin, whereas there are two qualifiers each time.

Stage one - places 7-10 from the league schedule compete and the top 2 qualify to stage two, Group B

Stage two - places 1-4 compete. The top two here go straight to the semi-final and the other two teams move to stage three.

Stage three - is competition between the losers of stage two, group A and winners from stage two group B.

The semi-final is between stage two, group A winners and stage three qualifiers.

*The semi-final and final are straight knock-out matches.

Scene One
Saturday Morning 11.12 am   Atkins Office

Andy Gill was mad on the Mustangs; so much so that he offered his services for nothing at Manager Tom Higson's obvious pleasure and thereby became what the club termed as the 'apprentice'.

Andy was standing outside the baker's shop which was somewhere between the stadium and the town's entrance. The young man, who wasn't so bright, was talking to one of his mates, sporadically looking down at his watch. On the last occasion he did, he gasped and shouted 'see you!' without reason or explanation to his friend.

With a quick glance left and right Andy sprinted across the road and at such a pace that he had to whirl round (making a motion like an aeroplane with his arms held out to keep his balance) jumping to one side in order to avoid hitting the brick wall he was heading towards.

"Watch it" shouted a couple as he leaped to one side to avoid colliding with them and other pedestrians.

Not stopping to turn around, he just shouted "sorry", so he could concentrate on his flight up Lord Percy Street in the rush to get back to the Atkins office, which was the last of those office buildings before the old ice stadium.

Reaching the door he quickly punched in his access code after swiping a key card to allow entry and forcefully pushed it open with both hands whilst clutching a small bag containing paperwork. He started to run up the stairs but hearing the door slam against the frame but not shut, he turned like a gymnast with both hands against the walls to steady himself and stepped back to floor level. He pushed the door closed and sprinted back up the stairs again. At the top he stopped abruptly, composed himself and turned 180 degrees around the wall on his left as if it mattered how he made his entrance, into the open plan office that had windows overlooking the main street.

"And where have you been, you know you were supposed to be back for eleven."
This was the rebuke from Mrs Higson, the secretary of the club.

It needs to be said here that while Vicki was still married in name to manager Tom the couple had, in fact, been unhappy for at least a year now and she seemingly avoided her husband. They still lived together but had grown apart and she was now (although it was not common knowledge) seeing Paul Hacking, the infamous brawling goon of the Mustangs team - who Andy looked up to - and there was little Tom could do about it at present. He had to keep them both on the payroll – at least to see out the rest of the season.

Andy strode up to the desk and was multi tasking, leering down Vicki's cleavage as he slumped down in a chair that faced her. As if he hadn't heard anything said to him he started to swivel round slowly and peered around at the room. The Manager's desk was adjacent to hers but was now considerably further away than it had originally been - typical of their real lives.

Tom's desk was by the front windows which Andy was looking out of, seeing the bookies down the opposite side of the street where he'd get Paul to put on a bet for him on the lottery, this kept the apprentice sweet and on Paul's side.

The street was full of shoppers and Andy could just make out his mate down the road still hanging around outside the bakers. "Maybe he thinks I am coming back" thought Andy.

His twirl in the chair brought him around to see the square glass patterned windows that were set in an old wooden structure to the rear of the room, which faced the front windows. It separated this area from the corridor behind, where there were four smaller rooms beyond - filing, meeting, store and then coaching room - which was the furthest from the staircase. The manager had this end room locked up as it contained the safe and only certain staff could gain entry using the same code system that Andy had just used to get in the building.

"SO...." bleated Vicki. "What about handing me the credit notes you have just collected?"

"Oh yeah" said Andy as he completed the spin of the chair. He stood up and peered once again at the secretary whilst trying to remain cool, asking if they were still leaving at the same time today in order to get to the game on time. Because he knew he'd have to stay till she left and lock the door with the code. Tom didn't trust her and certainly wouldn't leave a key with her.

"No, I've got a job for you which will take some time. It's very important and needs delivery of letters by 1.30pm at the latest. You'll find them in the back office left on top of the safe by Tom and each one invites our creditors to an important meeting which has to be held this week. So no delay and WHEN you have done that you can go to the match."

"Chuffing 'ell! I've only just got back." Andy retorted.

"No need complaining" came the reply, "you took so long dawdling about till now that you have left yourself little defence on that one. Get a grip and see as they get delivered or we're both in hot water...."

Andy's thoughts ran wild with the idea of him and her together in a hot tub but he was keen to get away and plonking the credit notes down on her desk, jumped up and quickly walked off. However, he hesitated by the entrance he had so calmly walked in by and gripping the old wooden frame turned to ask "Can I........'

"Noooooo....!" She bawled out to block out anything that Andy was about to request - which annoyed him immensely. So he pushed away from the wooden frame and walked off towards the end of the corridor, sneering through the patterned glass at her as he went.

Knowing that the security set-up had a camera, which took pictures of people going in and out from the end room, Andy looked up at it and with his thumbs set inside his ears and fingers spread and he blew a raspberry as the camera 'clicked.'

He let himself in by the code and as if forgetting what he was supposed to be doing leant against the large shelf to the left of him - which was just about shoulder height - and he peered at the three trophies which were displayed on it gathering dust.

Not having been a successful team, they were only in-house awards for 'Fans player of the year' to the left 'Players player of the year' in the middle and finally the 'Coach's award'. Andy squinted to read the names Hacking, Barton and Collins although he had read these on many occasions before today.

He wandered on to what was the side of the building, looking out of the windows ahead of him to the large office block opposite , viewing the people sitting and plodding at their keyboards for *'Merrivale's number one (and only) logistics company'*. He then looked below to see the same old view of green grass and a mass of brush that had grown over in time with the odd bit of litter blowing from Lord Percy Street and gathering between the 30 yard gap.

As if dusting the ledge below the windows he ran his fingers along them towards the back of the room until he finally came face to face with the three foot tall safe that sat on the floor, and then his mouth opened wide. But it was not the sight of anything to do with the safe but rather the pile of letters that had been left out to be distributed.

1, 2, 3....7, 8...12, 13, 14 he counted, all pre-addressed for him, "flipping ada!".....Andy sat down on a chair facing the trophies with his back to the safe.

With so many tables and chairs lined up facing the front, you'd think it was a school classroom. Andy looked like he was in lesson at his desk, laying out the letters in front of him in map formation in order to work the best delivery route. He would start by dropping off the furthest first and could end up back at the stadium as soon as possible. He wasn't that daft. Ha ha!

That done he jumped up and knocked back the chair accidently with his legs and stomped off, closing the room's door behind him. He momentarily forgot about the camera, 'click' it went off once more and the door buzzed behind him to confirm it had locked. Hearing this he turned round and – as he was about to let rip with a couple of fingers - he thought it best not to.

He turned, ran off and shouted "why can't he buy some stamps…?"…forgetting how urgent the letters were.

"Whoa there Gilly. You'll be going to the game after?" questioned Vicki

"Yes" he shouted back.

"Well, hand over your key card and I'll swipe us out when I go. It will save you having to come back again."

"OK," he said and flicked the key card which locks the front door and it landed on her desk.

The apprentice, equipment manager, security guard and the coach were the only ones who had one of these cards each (for here and M.A Enterprises) and the manager only visited there when someone was in working daytime hours. However, he'd usually get Andy to meet him after the second period in order to let him in but, in the rush to get away, Andy had forgotten about this. The code number was not enough to work the system, you'd also need the card for the door mechanism to work but Tom wasn't going to pay the £800 for an extra key card for himself.

Andy whispered over to Vicki, "5019."

She slithers the card into her jeans pocket and picked up the phone. She dialled a number and waited till the receiver could be heard being picked up at the other end of the line – at the same time hearing a slam of the front door at the bottom of the stairs.

"Hey gorgeous - have you left yet?" She asked.

"No, I am off soon," came the reply "but believe me when this is dealt with. You and me will be sorted and rid of him and this place. In a few months time we'll be living it up in a new home in sunny Nottingham babe!"

It was the sound of Paul's voice at the other end of the phone.

"Ok well get gone and see as you don't get caught" she replied, "Bye hunny!"

The phone was replaced but picked up again and another number dialled and the fly on the wall is the only one who hears.

"Hey, it's Vicki, can you do me a favour. I'm not feeling too well. Can you meet me in 10 minutes on Parliament Street behind the hairdressers?"

Bang, down goes the phone again. A few things were tossed into a small bag; perfume, lippy – once attired - and an assortment of beauty products from out of a drawer then up under her arm went the bag.

One last phone call to make: "Ring, ring, ring, ring"…there was no answer at first.

"Oh blast! That just about sums it …ah! Hi, its Vicki here. Not feeling too well and am off home….Andy has gone off with those letters and I'll lock up."

"What the….? What about the key card? Has Andy got it and what about…?" were a series of rushed questions from husband Tom.

"Hey – listen. I'll sort it. That's why I am telling you …. Just tell me you're coming here after the second period as you normally do…."

"Yes' as always but…."

"Ok…I'll get it sorted, OK…OK..." she said stingingly and slammed down the phone.

Five minutes later she had received a fax, scanned it and then turned everything off.

The phone rang back again but she ignored it and also ignored the mobile that went off in her bag as she 'clip clopped' down the staircase in the high heels that always announced her coming.
Seeing the door ajar yet again as Andy had – in his hurry to get out - let it slam once more, she raised her eyebrows.

"Anyone could get in with it like that….anyone….."

Estranged wife of Manager Tom, Presently dating Paul Hacking, goon of the Merrivale Mustangs Ice hockey team

Vicki Higson (neé) Wright

Andy Gill

Teenager who has some learning disabilities
Keen fan that helps out and is trusted by the manager to hold one of the few key codes that open the office building on Lord Percy Street

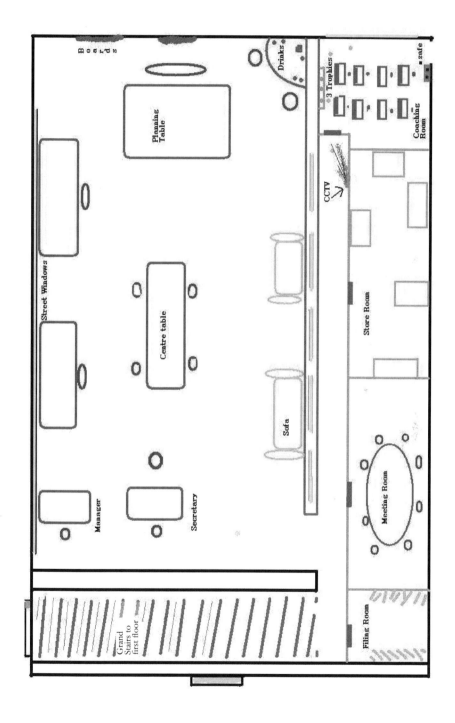

Scene Two
11.30 am

Early Arrivals

The main gates flew open but only for a few moments. Two cars sped from Lord Percy Street into the front drive of the Stadium then past the big bins at the far end. Not stopping for the main car park they carried on left round the curved blue wall where the sign proudly signalled 'Merrivale Ice Stadium' on the corner bend of the building and they continued down the space allowed at the rear between it and the rear boundary railings.

Near the bottom turn the cars reversed up against the railings so they were facing the stadium yet at an angle ready to drive off later back the way they had entered. It was some of the players who liked to get there early, joining them were some game stewards picked up along the way plus newly signed Will Weldon on loan being shown round the building by some of the team.

A few spaces further along near the next end turn (which would have got you back to the front) some cars had already been parked by the early morning cleaning staff. Cars would normally access out round that last turn but for the fact that it was cut off. With a pile of freshly dumped ice and a patchwork of wild bushes creeping up to the stadium wall filling the void they would instead have to drive back the way the players had just manoeuvred in. A gardener was definitely needed around the place but the Mustangs budget didn't stretch that far. It was unkempt and in places a bit smelly with the drainpipes in need of repair.

A cleaner who had made every effort inside to get the place ready for the day's game trotted up to her car carrying a few boxes and placed them in the boot. She had been emerging from one of the back doors, known as exit D, near the end of an early shift. But she'd be here a lot longer due to extra duties today.

"What you been nicking eh "said Adi Collins one of the players.

"Mind your own" was the answer from Geraldine Ellis the head of a two woman cleaning empire.......who then swiftly turned around and went back into the rink.

Just behind the cars were a few railings, that were not so perfectly aligned, so if you were small and agile enough you could slip through. But you'd have to get from Lord Percy Street first between the stadium and its neighbouring building Atkins Ltd to get there or via Atkins and the 'Chambers' logistics building but that was more open ground and someone may have seen you. Typical of the young boys, who were now gleefully playing war games, hiding from the enemy?

The boy's negotiated nettles and the mass of bushes that had been laid waste which was more exciting anyway than strolling past Chambers Logistics Company - anyway they had a mission. These local kids executed their plan perfectly like soldiers in enemy territory and today three of them were doing just that for a special reason and had slid between those faulty railings at the back.

But the doors to the complex were more of a 'mission impossible'. The heavy duty doors would lead you into a corridor under the seating which went all the way around the inside and these were impregnable for the kids, even the players had trouble yet a good kick would alleviate the problem, but the children didn't know this. Peering through the keyhole they'd be amazed at what they could see.

In full view of Neil Edwards one of the players arriving at the rink, they were looking through this keyhole to see if there was anything going on. Far too excited at what they were seeing to worry about anyone coming up behind them.

On hearing a muttering from Neil they scampered away to the ignorance of other players following on behind. There were a few hard knocks and kicks heard and then the throng who had just driven in disappeared inside. The young ones ran back soon after bags and sticks had disappeared into the dark interior, the children seeking possible entry if the door had not closed properly but they had missed their chance.

Now, Geraldine was bringing out another box of toilet rolls that she was going to sell off cheap, it was no wonder that the club was so badly off financially. This wouldn't help manager Higson's situation at all. He had threatened her with the sack because of a stock count that hadn't tallied only the month before, one of several discrepancies under Geraldine's care. He should never have taken her on with the poor record she had but she was cheap. Maybe she was ready to put in her notice and pinch what she could in the mean time or was she just dumb?

Exiting the door with box held out in front of her, Geraldine found these kids in her way as she huffed and puffed her way out.

"Hey, bugger off" she yelled as the door flung wide and clipped one of the lads who were backing up in surprise.

"Why misses, you scared I might tell on yer? "

Obviously the lad had over heard one of the players earlier mocking Geraldine as they had hidden in the undergrowth.

"Get out of here" She replied 'if I catch you here again I'll call the coppers on yer".

BANG! The steel door closed behind and the noise reverberated around the building as if the rivets of the titanic were ready to burst. The inside of the blue building was gloomily lit and nothing could hardly be seen either way you looked. There was a wide yawning gap of light straight ahead that gave away what was of interest to the kids. A staircase lifted up to the ice pads boards and an open door which showed the ice surface in its full glory and every so often the odd skater or two slipped by on the clean white carpeted mirage. It was this view that the young boys had seen before on their previous ventures after wading through the brush, scurrying up to spy on those inside, but there was not much going on today as it was far too early.

Players and stewards alike turned right and down this corridor and followed the path under the seating; this took you past some doors at times on the inner wall on their left, under the stadium seating, where very small stores were used as a dumping ground for unwanted items. As the corridor started to turn left at the end you first came upon exit/entrance C right behind the goal end and this was used by fans as an entrance when tickets had been bought in advance for ease of access.

Several yards later as the turn ended you came upon the unmarked front entrance and booking office where long standing workers Elaine Thompson and Maureen Smyth did customer service selling tickets and merchandise. The corridor then became long and straight again. The first aid room, after the entrance, opposite the booking office was better lit from several ceiling strip lights. Sat next to this was an equipment room and store then the major function room with a bar. Then two sets of changing rooms for the teams and then exit/entrance B (where fans also came in by) at the far end of the corridor before it started turning again to the rear of the building and exit A which was never really used.

You could walk the whole route and never meet anyone sometimes but on match nights when the gates opened up people would run round to chase up the inner stairs to take the best positions, though goodness knows why as attendances were falling dramatically.

The ice surface itself was the usual Olympic pad with team benches this front side near the function room. This was a blessing as the off ice officials could skip to the room's toilets in an emergency for a crafty fag between periods. The scorers table and penalty benches were of course opposite this nearer the back end of the building where players were coming in by.

At game time stewards - working in exchange for free admission - donned high-viz jackets and would let the fans in through doors B and C (as well as the small front entrance) but only if they had pre bought tickets. Only players and deliveries came in at the back door D where the local kids were challenging Geraldine's patience.

Why back door A never seemed to be used at all was a mystery to most, perhaps no one had a key or it was just stuck solid. The only other major aspect seen on the inside of this building was a small mezzanine landing above the main entrance and booking office, looking over the ice surface, where some strobe lighting and spotlights hung over the edge to shine its light upon the playing surface to greet the teams or at games end when players were collecting awards of beer.

It was up a slim and steep staircase that got you onto this level and Geraldine was huffing and puffing up it in order to get to the technicians.

"Chuffing ell Drew, I told you I'd see you at the back door 10 minutes ago. I'm running round like a fool here. Could have done with you, kept falling over some kids when taking that stuff out. You sorted with those cleaning products for the Sunday market yet? "

"Shhhh gal" said Andrew (Drew) Blatherwick, one of the older technicians, with finger stuck hard against his lips "remember where you are, this building transmits sound like a chuffing wind tunnel. Got it all sorted gal and I will have it all there by end of the second period. Just got to avoid his majesty, as you know, so keep your eyes open, I can't move anything under his nose for crying out loud."

The 'royalty' he referred to was owner Mark Atkin who had been floating around this morning checking on a new skate hire facility. Well - a storeroom that had been converted into one on the corridor bend near exit/entrance C.

Geraldine's teeth came into view as she showed her annoyance "But you said by the door at…"

"I know what I said but it's a change of plan now because we've had a problem with a spot light and I'm trying to do that at the same time. His lordship has been chewing my ear about it not 5 minutes ago. Be at exit D by early period start we'll start moving it on, stop panicking".

"So you say" a stern reply came.

With that Andrew turned and slid over to another tech guy - Chris Fielding - who was standing hands on hips as if he couldn't do anything without Drew and then, seconds later, both disappeared out of sight bending down to adjust wires to get the show ready for face off.

Geraldine on the other hand was pounding down the stairs muttering. Not too happy that the plan was behind schedule to relieve the club of a few more bottles of bleach and bags of cleaning cloths. Plus that fancy statuette figure sat in the store room gathering dust for all the years which she fancied for her own lounge at home. Talk about handling of stolen goods and playing with fire.
She was now off to a meeting where certain staff had been invited.

Exit D at the rear of the building used for entry by staff.

Adi Collins

Long serving player and one pin up boy for the admiring girl fans
Been a member of the side for seven years and gets along with most people
Helps out training younger players who are interested in the game

Geraldine Ellis

Local woman who has been a domestic hand for quite a few years
Has a history of working in areas that have had 'things' going missing

Neil Edwards

First choice net minder
Been 'off the rails' as regards form and temperament of late

Long term technician and friend of Geraldine Ellis
People trust or accept his decisions
Leads the other technicians on game nights
Keeps to himself until spoken to most of the time

Andrew Blatherwick

Technician but used as photographer on match nights
Does the leg work as regards contact with the printers for the club
Likes things to go smoothly or can start to complain. Definitely eager to help out but wants equal effort from all the other workers

Chris Fielding

One of the better views from around the Stadium, where the boys played

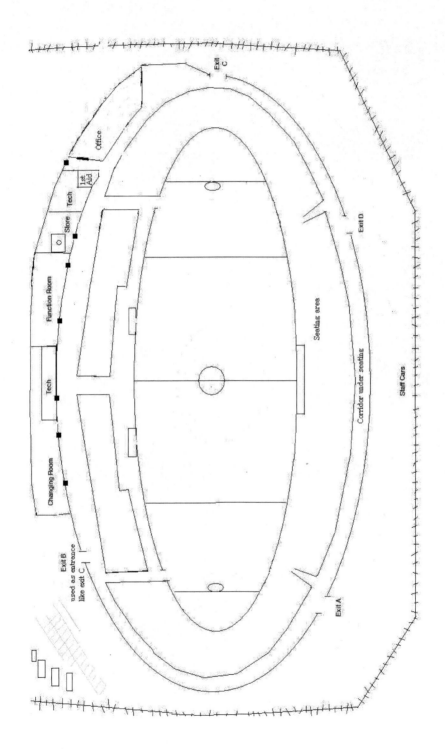

Exit C

Office

1st Aid

Tech

Store

Function Room

Tech

Changing Room

Exit B
used as entrance
like exit C

Exit D

Seating area

Corridor under seating

Staff Cars

Exit A

Scene Three
11.37am

The Build Up

Mustang players Bob Marshall and Wayne Pitchford were driving along Port Raven Way with Paul Hacking seated in the back with a couple of kit bags and several sticks - looking as happy as a man who had lost a ten pound note but found a fiver. He was transfixed by the scene ahead which bored him with every week that passed by.

"I'm looking forward to the end of the season. Had enough here and once its all over I've plans to move on." he said.

"You've said that so many times Paul" followed up Bob.

Then, as if to agree, Wayne pitched in saying "yeah, there's no money in this game anymore at our ages. What you think you're going to do, man?"

"I'll be rid of that annoying bugger of a manager for starters. Me and Vicki will hit the road. She says there's a big opening going her way in Sheffield. I'm gonna get a job in a casino 'cos she knows a few peeps round there. It's better than hanging around here for sure. Plus there's a nice pad ready to rent in Nottingham near by."

Wayne held a wince on his face, as Bob nodded in agreement and added.

"What in that place' god you'd need to be fed up of things here if that's your future plan, rather you then me."

"Like you said' came back Wayne in the debate....' got to rid yourself of her husband first. No way is he going to let her go with half his fortune tied up and considering his plight at the moment. Didn't you say they had to live together to keep the bills and things dealt with? He's not really over her yet Paul if ya ask me but he also doesn't want any confrontation."

"You bet boyo." replied Paul. "But if he gets in my way he'll be dead meat. "

But then, after a short pause, as if to cover the remark he continued

"But me and Vicki 'ave plans and don't want trouble either. Got a few business things to finalise chaps and that will ease a few worries. Then we'll start afresh up north."

"Hey what's that Paul?" asked Wayne "Anything I can add my expertise to".

"No thanks man, I got no chance of splitting this deal anymore. You can just drop me here, Wayne, and I'll see ya on the ice later. Just going to sort something out right now..... Hang on a minute - need my bag ".

The car had turned for the last time on its journey for Paul, still on Monarch Avenue and 100 yards short of Falconer square where he almost fell out of the side door as he clambered out. Slammed it shut and opened up the boot to reveal a kit bag and pulled on it to wrench it over and onto the road. Bob had got out, also dragging one of the sticks hidden amongst the bags inside of the car and passed it over to Paul.

"See you later Paul" he said but there was no reply.

Paul was looking out for someone and spotting the guy he was to meet up with ,threw his bag onto his back and pointed his stick at Chris Whittaker - the security man and head steward at the rink as if to state 'I'm on my way buddy'.

Bob and Wayne sped off down to Lord Percy street and waved out to Andy Barton , the hunk of the team who had been walking in but had been stopped on his way by a few female hockey fans for an autograph and if they were lucky a phone number.

"Well- Hi there, big boy. Got any action happening tonight?" came the first innuendo from Ligaya Damayo, a girl half his age.

'Yea' said Melanei Wagman her sister 'We want to see what you've got babe'

Trying to lighten the mood of the two hotties' remarks, Andy followed this with "Oh well got to see what the Scorpions bring with them, girls. Talk is that they are for the taking tonight and I'm up for a good fight too."

"Oh yeah?" the first girl replied, "Like a bit of rough, do ya?"

Realising that they were a tad too young and might pin him down further with more questioning, Andy changed tack.

Not wanting to get involved, he quickly threw in "OK then. Must rush!" and picked up his bag. He walked off but winked for the sake of keeping the girls happy. However, they were already showing glum faces and left as sharp as they had come with their chat lines and ran off to seek more adventure in Falconer square.

****

Fans were already milling around at this early stage of the day, weaving in and out of the paved ways from Lord Percy Street and Monarch Avenue into and out of the square.

The hockey bunnies were brushing past people to venture more excitement, but others, in no hurray, sat outside the cafes and small boutique shops just people watching.

The Square had a proliferation of planters, hanging baskets and quaint lampposts that gave a Parisian aspect but the local 'Caveman's' pub that overlooked the scene was the one building that looked completely out of place.

Stalwart fans Richard Archer and Jona Dolores were standing in the middle of the mayhem and were certainly "hyper" about the forthcoming game. Wearing scarves and carrying clipboards that would be used to pen stats and hold a programme, it was obvious to anyone where they were going. Richard was looking around for any well known faces from the club so he might glean some information for his new fanzine whilst Jona had her camera ready - just in case, because she was more into the web page she ran.

Some folks were out shopping and some were on their way home after an early bout in the town and now the hustle for ground space was getting a bit intense as each went there own way.

"Let's move over here" said Richard, so the two of them side-stepped toward the pub where clientele, with beers in hand, were stood chatting. The banter was giving out some interesting news and facts at times, one could hear mid sentence some complaint or excitement as people gave large their stories on the hockey game to come. It was not bad day weather - wise to be standing outside but everyone was looking at their watches, waiting a time to manoeuvre over the road. It would be cooler later after the game for sure though it was always a mild winter in these parts.

All of a sudden Jona saw Paul and Chris come out of the pub each with glass in hand. Both she and Richard wondered what Paul was drinking just before a game. You could almost see the fans ears stretched a little further to take in anything that might be of interest to them from one of their heroes - and maybe even get a chance to talk and get an interview for the fanzine they were putting out the following week.

Suddenly, money was seen to change hands from Chris to Paul and Jona caught a little gleeful remark from Chris saying that 'plans have been set'....Paul howled with laughter and leant towards Chris, as a response, punching him lightly in the chest.

"Yea - we've made a killing here."

The laughter was met by Chris who had his glass raised high as if to confirm the point.

"Dead right – going to make a killing."

"Wonder what that's all about" said Richard who whispered to Jona as she took a photo of the two guys.

****

The doors to the rink were pushed open and a small cry came from the queue that had formed at the entrance gates. Loud pumping music was heard as the DJ tested the sounds in readiness for the start of the entertainment. Tannoy announcements were being given the thumbs up by technicians, then a 'one two, one two' was heard and a line or two of a thumping track pounded out in the DJ's exuberance. He'd be milking the crowd later but loved the attention and didn't want to disappoint his public. So was rehearsing his stuff. "Hello folks it's your Saturday game DJ here ...Dave England."

Girls jumped up and down by the gate and talked excitedly to the boys - of which one was Bradley Brooks, another technician who was late coming in but, even then, he was still ahead of his normal time. He'd get caught up with the ladies pretending he knew a thing or two - more than he actually did - and then trying to arrange to meet them later. 'Meet me after the second period later babes' he'd say….but even he had to stand by as all bodies gradually parted and Andy Barton strolled in taking hand slaps on the back and all the 'hurrahs' and yo's as he went.

Both he and Bradley - who hurried along behind - strutted up to the buildings main entrance which was, in fact, just a dual glassed door in frame.

The fans with pre-booked tickets more likely went to one of the two larger doors to either side of the main entrance in order to get in. Exit/entrance B to the right or exit/entrance C just before that mountain of dumped ice at the end of the stadium to the left. With these tickets they'd get in quicker.

However fans with no tickets would line up to buy them at the small front entrance from the two ladies at the glass windows when entering.

A chorus of "why are we waiting" started up as more fans started to move over from the square to get in the mix ready to penetrate the old place in a rush to get their personal favourite seating area. It would be some time though before the gates were opened properly as regular stewards Antoine and Tony began closing them up again.

Ice stadium and neighbouring Chambers Logistics Company is seen behind. The smaller hockey offices ATKINS 'unseen here' lies between. These are exit/entrance B (to the left) and exit A which was nearer the rear of the building stuck shut

Chris Whittaker

Hard case security man and Key card holder to the Atkin building. Helps out regards handyman duties in all the buildings operated by team owner Mark Atkin

Paul Hacking

Team goon who is dating the Managers wife Not the brightest person but gets no hassle from anyone for certain. Not getting much Ice time and believes the manager has something to do with it. Had enough of living in Merrivale

Wayne Pitchford

Average' Joe bloggs' who 'does his own thing' One of those things is his unhealthy interest in woman Joker of the Mustangs pack, who is well liked by the team

Bob Marshall

Newer member of the team but fitted in well. Lodges with team mate Wayne and is keen to make his mark in the team

Andy Barton

Likeable hunk used by the club in sponsorship promotional duties

Ligaya Damayo

Regular fan with sister Melanei
Miss Mustang 2019
Hangs around with the players when the players are interested in hanging around her

Melanei Wagman

Younger sister of Ligaya
Another hockey bunny intent on getting to know all the 'good looking' players

Richard Archer

Fan who likes to be involved
Knows a lot but is it all fact?
Statistician, fanzine editor

Jona Dolores

Jona, fan and friend of Richard
Amateur Photographer and runs an unofficial
website

Bradley Brooks

Young technician who is a bit lazy, not always
'on the job'
Doesn't like being told what to do

Dave England

The clubs DJ
Works for anyone in Merrivale but enjoys the
chance to 'work the mic at games.

Scene Four
11.50am
A Staff Meeting

"Come on come on, for goodness sake. If I can get here on time then why can't you?" were the unwelcoming words from Tom Higson who stood at the top of a flight of stairs in the main office building (M A Enterprises) on Port Raven way.

It was a single open-plan room, with sofas and fancy furniture which made visiting sponsors comfortable when Mr.Atkin was pampering guests clinching deals.

"Sorry, Mr.Higson" replied Chris Phillips, the team coach "was making sure young 'Gilly' was sorted with those delivery notes you wanted going out today, boss. He was given the job by Vicki and he looked as though he was very confused. I was just coming over......" - Chris held his arm out wide to elaborate – "Saw him in the street and all he was concerned about was getting to the match on time."

Tom stood tall and motioned towards the back of the room. It was Mark Atkin team owner who was none too pleased the way things were going and was here to state the obvious: if things didn't improve he would be closing the team down at the end of the season.

"Good afternoon …ladies and gentleman." said Mark sternly

He was referring to coach Chris and manager Tom as well as the two cleaners - Geraldine and her assistant Sandi Stephenson - plus David Temple the equipment manager, who had sat down with a coffee taken from the plush drinks machine. There were about ten others too, who were still there from an engineers monthly meeting which tried to eradicate problematic electric and maintenance problems. Asked to listen in and spread the word.

Right now Mark Atkin wanted to talk to the main culprits who he understood were letting him down and these people would get the message across to everyone else back at the stadium.

Atkin continued…"First of all, may I remind you that I am the boss" – then, after a short silence…. "And the reason I am here is to say that we are trying to see the season out in as profitable a position as possible. But if the balance sheet does not tally and put us into the black, the old building on Percy Street will become the next supermarket in town."

"You mean 'Dasco's'!" interrupted Sandi. "I've heard they are interested. Oh - I could get my usual without running up Yarmouth Street - its miles away up there and hubby ….." She stopped as if to think long and hard, looking around at all looking at her and then decided to shut up. Eyes rolled to the backs of heads and Tom and Chris fleetingly closed theirs in dismay.

Atkin continued directing his words at Sandi, although they were meant for all of them.

"If you want to lose your job - then fine! But for the sake of all - and my bank account - I'd ask that you concentrate on the present day. Mr.Higson has informed me that things are awry with everything at present. I know that the buildings old and we need to sort out some problems but we - err, I mean *I* cannot do that with little cash. The leagues money pot has held firm as regards handing out any more cash until the end of the season and I want to be part of that - but if we can't get there I'm done for. Too much has been spent on this town by me already. Cloth has to be cut and belts tightened".

Coach Chris asked "Forgive me, Sir, but what of the community and the shops that survive on local sales? The big concern would kill them off. It would also be in direct competition with your own butchers and fruit and vegetable products on Knight Avenue."

"That's no concern of mine chap; I'll be long gone by then." came the reply. "As I've just said, I have held this town up enough with my contributions. It's time for me to think of myself and, while people are not supporting this team, I can't worry about it if that be the case. I need to keep these sponsors and that won't happen if I can't pay the bills and get to next season. So let's get this all sorted out at our end and make it to March in order to get this money, which will keep everybody's heads above water. The Knight Avenue outlets are fine. It's this chuffing big blue stadium that's not keeping up. The land's more useful but I'd like to see the stadium stay".

With that he turned and left. That was it, simple and to the point.
This was a cue for Tom to take over.

"That leaves me with orders to give a final warning to you all. The new room being used on the corridor for storage and hire of skates needs to be replenished and cleaned up by Geraldine and Sandi. The skates are to be sharpened and repaired and placed into that room. Technicians will sort out our problems of the zamboni and lighting in the mean time. Spread the word to the rest of the staff that this is Mr Atkins' last words on this one and I know that he means it. Let's see some improvement!"

Looking at David Temple straight in the eye he continued "Long have I told you about the running of things inside of that building. It is your responsibility to make preparation for the players and we are not getting that from you. I am aware of the number of things being asked but you can prioritise. You have that sharpening and repairs to do on those public skates and today you will be doing those straight away and during the game, they have to be ready for Sunday's session."

Turning to the cleaners he says, "Now, you two need to get back there and sort the public skate hire area for tomorrow. It has to be done now or tonight after the game. I asked for this to be done a long time ago and when David has the skates dealt with, they can be put in their racks accordingly. We can't do that until you lot get on with this."

"What's wrong with everyone?" he continued, "we should all be working together as an *off ice* team but this team is letting down the *on ice* boys. Without both it all falls apart. People won't come in and spend money the way it is. Match results are bad but money needs to come from another source if the hockey fans are not turning up.

Skate sessions have to be improved upon. Our part is to make good the equipment and its housing has to be better. Please see to this."

David was patiently waiting to chip in and made ready a daring comment. "What about the wage rise we haven't had plus that bonus from season's start?"

"Bonus? Bonus? For what? We are not showing anything for it" was an enraged reply from Tom.

At that moment, the door flew open and Bradley Brookes appeared up at the top of the stairway and apologised saying that he had gone to the stadium instead and had forgotten about the meeting. Tom suggested he start to use his brain for once and stop day dreaming.

Bradley tried to save himself.

"I was helping to sort out the lighting earlier with Drew Blatherwick but Chris Fielding was there doing it. I just thought you meant ME when you said to help out with the lighting the other day."

A short pause before Tom came back into the conversation.

'Gawd help us! We can now see what's going wrong and why we should concentrate more...Right Coach - I want a word with you about our league position."

Pointing at the cleaners he said "You two - get down to the skate room. And you – Bradley - NOT Chris Fielding, I want you to get back to the stadium NOW and join the other technicians to help with the zamboni. It's a bit too late me telling you what's needed from you anymore if you're not listening; it's a final warning for you. Just be told for the last time - get here to work on time! And, David, I need a word before you go."

Motioning David across to him, Tom lowered his voice and said.

"I need the parcel addressed to me which is sat in your equipment room dropped into the Percy Street Atkins office by the safe - sometime today. But with regard to anything else the main importance is to get those skates done."

"But what about the bench? I run the bench on match nights - door, sticks, who's doing that…"? came a frustrated bellow.

"No worries, I will sort it, Steward Antoine Marie-Jeanne will deal with that."

David was not amused…"No way! Him …?'He'll ruin everything!"

"Forget it" came a sharp reply "its happening…. Ladies! Start wielding those brooms and dusters, please, and – Geraldine - I need a word about toilet rolls later, if you please. See me at Percy Street office at second periods end before you do anything else. Remember there has been a warning of sackings by Mr.Atkin and, believe me, I have spoken to other individuals, not just you lot. No one is safe. Be warned."

"Permit me to ask one last question" ventured David.

"No" came the abrupt response, "get that package over to the coaching room and see to those skates!"

Tom beckoned to the coach with a wave and a mention of his name…."Chris…"

Everyone stormed out, Bradley at a stroll but muttering, speaking as if others were listening to him. Within time all had scurried down the stairs as Sandi's husband had his van outside waiting to take them all back and off to do their duties leaving two loan figures in the room upstairs. Tom softly motioned to the coach. He had the chance to talk now rather than later in the day.

"We have been told or - should I say - Mr.Atkin has been advised that, should we get the quarter-final slot, then Carlton Scorpion Kenny McKie is interested in finishing the season with us. He is obliged by his contract to see out terms with Carlton but only to the end of their cup run. So - if we dispose of them today, we could be onto a winner here considering our additional cup points from the handicap system. Can't say too much - but Kenny wants a personal shift out of their club. Don't think he'll be too eager to score on us today".

Tom put his finger to his nose tapping it to indicate a 'keep this under your hat'.

Coach Chris could do little but accept this and nodded, while moving on to another subject.

"But I want to be able to use Paul more in games, Tom. I know how you feel about him but it's hurting us to leave him on the bench so much. I can't keep taking this money off you also. You know what the boss just said - we need to get to next season for sure. The likes of Mick Holland at the paper keeps asking why a points scoring enforcer is not being used and you're also claiming that we need points in the league table. If you want Kenny we need to assure a win today"

Tom's face dropped and the mild manner with Chris changed.

"Listen, Phillips! When you needed help with that claim on your house during that fire… The insurance would not have paid out unless my brother had signed those papers, mate. Don't want to hear anymore about it, do as I say…'

Tom stuffed a few more twenties from his pocket into Chris's hand with force.

"And see that the ink on the paperwork dries before you say anymore about it…or else!"

Tom was angry. His problems with the hockey and also with his wife were not good. Paul was interfering in his life and he was trying to get back at him by blackmailing Chris. Things were building up inside of him. He had not been in such a bad way, nobody knew the half of it and he hadn't been himself the past few months.
Losing friends - or what could be termed friends - and now it could be his wife.

As much as he hated the situation he believed he could get her back. He needed the team to survive the season. He knew Atkins was going to sell the building and grounds to Dasco's anyway and the promise of a 'bung' from the boss - with the end of season sponsors money that was presently deferred – it would aid his plans. This meant he could afford to take Vicki away from all of this and give something he had always promised. Something that tyrant Paul could not afford - a home in the Philippines. But that wouldn't happen unless he could keep the team going until March.

"I'll be back in the rink's office at two thirty."… Were Tom's last words before he too left the room, hurrying down the stairs.
The coach looked sternly into Tom's back as he scurried off'.
"Is that a fact, mate? "

Manager and devotee to owner Mark Atkin
Runs things his way which is not always appreciated by others
Wife Vicki is secretary of the club and they are on a rocky marriage at present

Tom Higson

Coach
Takes direct orders from Tom.
Also has a key coded card
Third year in the job, another local man

Chris Phillips

Owner
Has 'fingers in many pies' with an office beside the stadium and other major projects are worked upon a few minutes away at M A Enterprises on Port Raven Way.

Mark Atkin

Assistant cleaner to Geraldine Ellis
Not been with the club long
Not a good listener and a bit forgetful but happy go lucky

Sandi Stephenson

Equipment manager to the team
Supports team coach and is the stadiums skate hire chief

David Temple

Outside 'M.A. Enterprises' on Port Raven Way, where the meeting was held

Scene Five
12.15pm

Pre Game

'Welcome once again to the big blue stadium that is the home of the mighty Merrivale Mustangs. Take your seats and please be vigilant of any puck that may fly tonight when the game is in motion. Don't leave your seats when play is in action and - most of all sit back and enjoy yourselves!"

"And yes…here they are ladies and gentlemen, boys and girls. The lads in Black and Orange and sponsored tonight by 'The Legend Bar', The Merrivale Mustangs led by Captain Gary Stefan……"

"I'm your host Dave England and please, please come and give me any music requests, celebratory announcements or money …ha ha. I will mention it, visit it or even spend it! …It's going to be a hell of a game."

Dave England slams on a record that elevates the noise in the building. Cheers and boos ring out as almost immediately in the background the visiting Carlton Scorpions slip onto the ice but without spectacular razzmatazz.

Regulars shout out the names of their favourites.

"Come on Molin, do your stuff and let's stuff em!" bleated stalwart Richard Archer as his compatriot Jona Dolores was busily marking down names and details for the match statistics that would come later.

With an excited wave Melanei Wagman, who was sitting at the front, screamed out "Hiya Steve" and blew him a kiss as she tried to attract 'Pelletier's attention. Though the sight alone of her jumping up and down more likely caught the attention of neighbouring male fans seated around, who would gladly have accepted any interest for them instead, as they ogled her whilst she banged on the plexi-glass.

"Who hoo, Adi" was the next cry as Collins wheeled around the ice, to which he gave a wave but was still unsure of who it was he had acknowledged as he whizzed past.

Melanei's sister Ligaya Damayo sat calmly playing with her hair and being more receptive of the glares coming their way from the gentlemen who were sitting closest and who were leering at them both, less interested in the pre-game formalities.

"Give me an M" bounded from Dave's microphone …and a U, S, T, A.N.G.S was a request, which got a return shout from Block Four's 'Mad crew'. The non seated block residents didn't really care what the score was half the time as long as enforcer Shaun Yardley threw his weight about. This time they decided to call upon Tom Norton to give them a wave. But Tom was uninterested and skated over to the bench to receive a towel for a wipe of the brow under his helmets protecting visor.

"Bloody ell, he's sweating already!" was a discerning comment from Bradley who was by now actually where he should have been (post work on the zamboni) on the gantry high up with the other technicians still fighting with the lights on the mezzanine. Then 'ping' they suddenly came on and some fans cheered in sarcasm because they knew this was a regular fault. Later they would also cry for their 'money back' once the team went a goal behind. These were the usual game moaners, who unfortunately sat near the mezzanine and threw comments up all afternoon if the lights went on the blink.

"Move over" Bradley ushered, with an elbow to Chris Fielding who was now bedecked with cameras round his neck in the role of photographer for the game.

"Are you kidding me" said Chris, "Just keep that shut and do some work" was his advice.

This upset Bradley who got very animated and caused fans from below to look up as the two jostled with each other on the verge of an off-ice brawl.

"For goodness sake, I've just got the lights working, stop causing a rumpus or we'll have to do all this again and we all want to see the game!" said fellow technician Drew, who was getting a bit anxious with both of them especially as Bradley was backing up into him.

"Get out of the way yourself, Bradley. You're no use even when you're here, kid."

Hearing this Bradley stormed off down the stairway and proceeded to strut around the building in earnest to seek female company.

It was all kicking off which was nothing new here on game day with the usual mayhem of incidents.

Geraldine by now was trying to get the attention of Drew and was pointing towards the other end of the ice once she had caught his eye, then gave him a 'thumbs up'. Drew was making out that he had not seen her, not wanting to draw more attention. He just wrapped up a few cables, laid them down and nudged Chris on the shoulder saying 'I'm off a while'.

"Hope it's not for long, Drew. I am sat here taking photos as ordered, but can't deal with the lights on my own." explained Chris.

"Don't worry, it's sorted I found the problem we've had for weeks. I will be back by mid period," was the reply. Then he clambered down to Ice level and then the corridor below that.

David Temple was just coming out of his store between the function room and the first aid room. Clutching a parcel he had just picked up to deliver as requested.

"You busy as well?" asked Drew as Geraldine joined them a split second later.

"Too right, got to start sharpening those skates for you Geraldine and it will take me all game long. I'm pissed off with that, as his royal highness, Higgs Boson also wants this parcel delivering to the office next door …bleeding cheek. I'm going to do that now because I really want to do some skates then catch the last 5 minutes at end of the game before churning out more skates. Also see if Antoine is doing the job proper on the bench. That's really wound me up. Next thing Ant will have my equipment job and I'll be out on my ear, so better I get this parcel thing done before I've forgotten."

"Ok, mate." said Drew "Just do me a favour - you never saw us. Me and Geraldine have something to do prior to game start, must go."

"Alright, as long as you tell him you did see me doing a good job taking this parcel over before the game, ha ha. I will be back in the equipment room in 10 minutes anyway, so I never saw you two all game."

Then he winked to complete the conversation.

****

Over by the players bench Antoine was doing a fine job arranging sticks and water bottles, leaving players requirements in place as directed having been given the job instead of David Temple. He was happy at ice level for a change, instead of being stuck in block 3 stewarding middle ice in front of the function room.

Steward Tony Grainger had been passed on information to swap roles with him at management's request for this game and thus move into block 3 from his usual favoured block 6. Tony wasn't best pleased himself as he rather liked his own placement, mainly because security man Chris - who he didn't much like - was around block 3 area, wandering between the top end exit/entrance B and this bottom first aid room corner. Chris would normally give Tony some hassle and mock him just because he could. Tony thought he was a nasty man and avoided him if possible because he didn't want any trouble, though he could be a cheeky joker himself playing tricks on people. Chris Whittaker just got in the way.

Players gradually skated off to a few cheers but also a few groans.

"Make sure you hit 'em this week, Nikolov!" came a shriek from the crowd, as players headed to the dressing room. The players could either not hear the disgruntled fan or just chose not to react.

Danny Scott got a better reception though with applause as he left.

"Danny, I love you!" rang out as he trotted off the ice, because he was on form and seen as the one putting most effort in lately. But if tonight's game were to end up in a single goal defeat again there would be more negative comments for sure.

Frankie Killen and Graham Waghorn were the last two to make their way to the dressing room. Graham waited on Frankie by the boards because he wanted to be last off the ice surface in the suspicion that he'd have a bad game otherwise.

This was his usual routine but Frankie was keeping him waiting as he was wielding his stick to some applause , taking in the atmosphere after getting as much practice in as possible in case he was called up for action.

The stream of bodies coming into the stadium was slackening off by now. But the attendance was a lot better than the last few games which was promising, though you could still see big gaps between fans, especially at the farthest point from the main entrance. A less popular area round exit A which became a choice for the 100 away fans decked in Blue and White.

David 'Stef' Litchfield, the announcer, was ready to give large the particulars of team names and numbers ably assisted by Dee Shaw at his side who was setting up the game sheet ready for penning goals and penalties alike.

Sitting close behind in the crowd - just in case they wanted to query anything – were Mike Appleton, chair of the writers association and local writer Stewart Roberts who was doing his latest piece about the rise in popularity of the game. Stewart was one of a very few who gained free entry to matches because of his efforts to entice locals to come along. He wrote the team's yearbook and had many other projects like the home programme and trading card production. Both he and Mike would be planning on a media guide for the new sports organisation and were partied to a new governing body that would seek to promote the sport in the right places. The Mustangs owner also wanted them on board in or around Merrivale so he could keep tabs on what was happening.

Opposite them on the other side were Ronnie Nichol and Jim Lydon who were not new to Merrivale but not regulars here on game days. They were statisticians to the sport and Mark Atkin was wondering why they were here tonight. They held some weight as they were the ones who had introduced the new consortium to the sport. So much was happening with this new era in hockey and Mark planned to go over and speak with them later. Presently he was sat in his usual seat near the off ice officials benches with trusty servant Dave Hallam around him to cater for his needs. Dave Hallam also had to listen out for tannoy announcements that asked for his assistance as he was also the first aid person on site in case of player injury or public need.

Just as the music entertainment was building up towards the start Drew and Geraldine could be seen swiftly edging through the seats over at the far end with the Scorpion fans, moving towards exit door A. Security man Chris Whittaker was moving left to right over from that way towards them, then started to engage into banter with both before continuing on his own way again. Drew and Geraldine dipped into the exit concourse below the seats and Chris towards the main hub of fans mid ice and then disappeared down a stairway from block 2 to the corridor underneath. Steward Tony in block 3 saw all this and wondered whether Chris was on his way over to him or just might, hopefully, be going elsewhere. Either way, he felt uncomfortable.
To the tune of 'Hockey town Merrivale' sung by local band 'Trip' Dave England spoke over microphone to say that the game had been delayed a short while because of the zamboni needing attention.
The crowd whistled at this news showing contempt but responded with a mix of clapping in time to the music soon after because it was near time for the drop of the puck.
Then, all of a sudden, the zamboni sped into view and Dave England threw up his hands as if to say 'I look a right twat now saying the game was delayed'.

Tony Grainger was so uptight about seeing Chris appear from up his exit stairway that he stood back, but he needn't have worried as Chris was far too interested in what he himself was doing. Tony was able to hear things mentioned by Chris who had lent over to people sitting in that area.

"I'll see you as before, no problems with tonight"…It meant nothing to Tony, yet he would hear a few things, more during the game which would impact on a few thoughts.

****

There was an on ice presentation of a bunch of flowers to an elderly couple by player Rhys McWilliams, selected to hand over these as a thank you and best wishes for their many years support and in conjunction with their 50th wedding anniversary.

They had met each other at hockey games years ago and both could also recall that the interior was still the same as it was today. Steve Butler, another player in attendance handed over a present wrapped up and added that "all 50-year followers of the Mustangs would get the same treatment of course." No one knew, however, if he was being real or taking the 'mickey'.

At this imminent time of game start, Dave Hallam was on an errand for owner Atkin, off to ask Ronnie and Jim (the stats men) if they would join Mr Atkin for a drink at the end of the period. On the way over, Dave noticed the figures of Maureen Smyth and Sandi Stephenson leave the booking office and walk into the first aid room. He wasn't overly worried about this but wondered what it was all about. One was an office clerk and the other a cleaner. Both had the giggles as they entered. Then simultaneously, crashing through the main entrance from the grounds outside was Elaine Thompson (looking flustered) who really should have been in the office herself. Dave had to think. Had someone had an injury? Should he enquire now or get to see the statisticians before it was too late?

From the smells of burning, either from the function rooms of over cooked hot dogs or gloves having been dried from hair dryers, to frantic squeals of delight or shouts of excitement, plus the sight of doors closing for probably the last time. People started to get that feeling that hits you each week. The puck will drop and it's a new game and a new chance. Forget last week's game; this is the one to win. This is where things will change. This is Merrivale's time and moment to hit back.

The main entrance to the building

In that split second, Dave decided to get the invite over with first before the puck was dropped then drop into the first aid room himself. He walked past the sounds of grinding skates from the equipment room and smells of player liniment wafting down the corridor as he skirted around fans who were in a hurray to get to their seats. He then jumped up the stairs to ice level meeting up with Tony Grainger and explained that he wanted to point out Ronnie and Jim so Tony could aid them to the function room at period end. To offer them a courtesy drink as Mr Atkin was going to be coming that way to meet them.

Then Dave slipped among the crowd apologising to some as he sidled in front to lean over to speak with Ronnie and Jim and invite them personally as Mr Atkin had proposed. They accepted so Dave made his way back down to the corridor with thumbs up to Tony as he pointed them out.

Making it back to the first aid room, he tried the door and knocked but it was locked - which was very unusual. However, rather than make it his job to search out the key, because he had lent his to equipment guy David, he thought he'd ask questions later of the ladies to see if all was OK.

There was no answer to a final knock so he decided not to worry as maybe they were needing privacy and surely the door would be back open later. Right now he wanted to pass on the good news to Mark Atkin and get ready for the game himself.

From the outside of the building the roar of the crowd, led by block 4 could be heard. It gathered momentum as face off time approached. The referee and linesmen were winging onto the ice to a chorus of boos. Particularly the referee, as Gordon Pirry was the match official last time out against the Scorpions. Fans didn't like the idea that he could ruin the chance of this cup run. He had blown up for a penalty on star player and captain Gary Stefan seconds from time last game they saw him and had awarded a penalty shot, Mustangs losing because of it. He had better keep his silly calls out of the game today.

Antoine Marie-Jeanne

Steward
Would like to be part of the off ice support team

Dave Hallam

First Aid man for both team and the public 'Gofer' for owner Mark Atkin on match days

Tony Grainger

Steward
Looks after entrance C and the end of stadium seating in block 6 normally
Has bad history with security man Chris Whittaker

Elaine Thompson

Booking office worker
Will do anything for anybody, a 'giving' person
Enjoys her job and been there a few years as a local supporter before this job

Maureen Smyth

Booking office worker and friend of Elaine
A family woman, who has a good reputation though she does not have to work, as she likes to engage her mind

Scene Six
1.10pm   First Period

No. Dave England was right. The game would be delayed. The linesmen were calling the players back into the dressing rooms but nobody could understand why. Some fans were shouting at the officials whilst others were holding their hands up in disbelief. But, whatever it was, Chris Fielding was happily snapping away pictures on the mezzanine and the lights were fine. No need looking up there for problems.

Suddenly a working zamboni slipped onto the playing surface and made its way towards block 1 and moved around the edge of the ice by the boards doing some sort of clean up job. The referee was being very strict as regards the state of the ice before any puck was going to be dropped. The two linesmen began to check the nets and referee Gordon Pirry stood pointing for where he wanted the ice surface cleared. How long was this going to take?

****

Back in the home dressing room, players were shuffling around taping sticks, having a drink or doing some small task to fill in the time as the coach Chris Phillips paced around in circles pointing at individuals and reiterating once again what he wanted of them. Andy Barton nodding with every sentence yet Bob Marshall was looking towards Paul Hacking with eyes rolled to the top of his head, Paul sending him back a similar facial grimace.

Chris was only doing the best he could in the meagre time available to get across what coaches wanted to say. He was pointing out the importance of the game and reminded them of the benefits of marking the Scorpions' left winger.

"But the man to worry about is Kenny Mc Kie," chipped in Andy.

A quick reply came back from Chris. "Not this game. Concentrate on the others and believe me, we'll be fine. "

Suddenly, David Temple burst into the room and handed over some skates that had been requested by Adi Collins and set about helping him unlace those he already had on - in order to get immediate use of the better pair, instead of having to wait until the first period interval.

Walking out of the room, coach Chris turned to face everyone and raised one finger up to add a final comment just as the buzzer sounded outside noting the game was ready to start.

"That's another thing, guys. Wayne is missing at present - searching out a finger guard. So fill in at the back till I say so."

"Not my fault..." said David, who was lacing up the last part of a boot.

"I know, David," replied the coach. "Wayne took it upon himself to go to the first aid room knowing you were stuck in the equipment room."

At that, all the players got up en mass and moved to the door in the hope of getting the game underway this time. David went back to his job as the players filed out one by one to a few cheers from nearby fans who were close to the corridor stairway. Then Antoine – who had been standing quietly in the background – followed suit through the door, struggling with a pile of spare sticks. Last out of the door was a lethargic Neil Edwards (net minder) bringing up the rear muttering away as usual.

****

The clock on the wall said 1:20pm and the game was behind the original face off time. Players circled until a whistle was blown. Like a bench clearing brawl in reverse, all players quickly scrambled over the boards - bar the first line who squared up. New recruit 'Will' was stood by the boards and would be running the door as his paperwork had not got here in time, so would miss this game.

Neil Edwards in goal stood tall, Graham Waghorn seemed psyched, whipping up the crowd with fellow rearguard Tom Norton who was already pretty focused.

Up front were Angel Nikolov, Johann Molin and Captain Gary Stefan who was talking to all of his line mates for the last time.

On the bench – as expected - by himself as well as the rest of the team was Paul Hacking spitting onto the ice and glaring at the Scorpions players - as was Shaun Yardley in mean fashion.

Standing up and making direct eye contact with their minder was Daniel Scott. Was this to be a good game? - The day that would bring about positive headlines in tomorrow's paper from Mick Holland? Or was this just the hype that was on show before another sad statistic in the loss column... hailed amid jeers and frustration? Like had been said, beat Carlton then push on after that. Things had to change, even if the stadium was still mechanically woeful.

From the off it was a scrimmage with no real identity as to which side would make the first real move on the other. Play was centre ice with body against body with the likes of Rhys McWilliams and Adi Collins in there for the action. Wayne Pitchford had arrived back to the bench and, as he did second liners were now in the mix, with Steve Butler and Wayne taking matters into their own hands and pushing the play up ice. The game ebbed and flowed a bit until one of the Scorpions took a penalty for rubbing his glove in Molin's face a bit too much for the referee. It included a push down onto the ice afterwards and then players got into a tangle because of this.

In the enclosed bench area, players got animated about the harsh treatment they thought they were getting from Scorpions.

****

'What the hell do they think they can get away with'?

'It's our barn lads and we'll just have to remind them of that'

'I'll take a piece of that number nine for starters, I will'

****

"Two minutes for interference" called Stef Litchfield, the announcer. Then the first line jumped back on for the power play.

All went well until Daniel Scott was called 25 seconds later for a tripping infringement. Big hits were made and during all this Graham Waghorn took a nasty cut to the cheek from a bad high stick….."Two plus Two for accidental high sticks"….this was now a big chance over half way through the period.

With Scott due back on seconds later, the face off was won by Norton who made a bit of space for himself and dispatched a nice pass that split through all players to Stefan who quickly whipped it into the minder's glove that instantly peeled out back onto the ice.

A stick from the minder flipped this away to his right but incoming Molin at pace slapped it straight into the 'onion bag'. The strength of his shot tore the net back with such a force that the puck pinged back and ended up under the goalie that still lay strewn on the white stuff after he had thrown himself to clear the original shot.

GOAL and 1-0 to the home side after a good start, scoring at 16.54.

The game got heated and the clock stopped every few seconds – or so it seemed - as first Scott then Barton and Pitchford got into scuffles. Coach Chris sent Paul Hacking on finally and he immediately found himself in mid-clash with a Scorpion. The pair of them headed straight for the boards with neither wanting to give way to the other.

In the Mustangs' own defence zone directly in front of the Carlton away fans, they clattered into the boards with sticks high and elbows hitting the plexi-glass at the same time.

Shards of the stuff rained down on them as the panel disintegrated. It would require a short delay to have this repaired, with brush and pan and new glass made ready it wouldn't be long before the game could restart. In the meantime, the players took advantage of the break.

With supporters cheering hard and Melanei and Ligaya adding shrieks of delight, it seemed ultimately to be Merrivale's best first period of the season. The block 4 crew got into singing mode as the players skated over to their benches. Noise was everywhere, with Dave England asking for more and super fans like Jona and Richard responding as asked. Jona was clicking away with her camera for a few vital pictures for the forthcoming fanzine and website as well as trying to write down in her match programme. It was all go.

Chris Whittaker (security) trotted down a few steps to ice level and spoke with Paul by the boards. The noise was so deafening that it was hard to understand that anyone could actually hear one another at this time. Tony Grainger had his beady eye on Chris, though, and, whilst asking someone to stop banging on the block 3 plexi-glass (to avoid another delay), he was half encapsulated into listening to the players remarks near him. This didn't seem like hockey talk to him.

"I'll kill him!" by Paul was rebuffed by Chris "No, I'll sort it, you keep cool..."

With play back underway and things a little more sedate for the remainder of the period, the score remained the same at the first break. Steve Pelletier had not even got on the ice yet because things had gone so well. All the others came out of the first with pats on backs and broad smiles. Was this going to go their way after all - or would this turn against them?

Back on Lord Percy Street the last of the shoppers were making their way home.

Scene Seven
1.42pm

First Interval

There seemed to be a hurried affair going on outside exit/entrance B. Technicians Chris Fielding and Bradley had been called into action. Even first aider Dave was pulled in to get pieces of damaged plexi-glass carried outside towards the large bins in the car park. Proof - if needed - that the club was run on a shoe string. Chris was originally bemoaning the absenteeism of Bradley until he had emerged. But it was not long before Chris was complaining again and asking where Drew was.

Manager Tom suddenly turned up, mentioning he wasn't too pleased, as he ushered them on with hands motioning them to hurray up. Tom himself had been roped into looking after the lights on the mezzanine, after Drew had been reported missing. So, again, Chris Fielding stated how both of them seemed to be running from one end of the building to the other. Tom however, was not listening at all, just barking orders and then waiting for them outside to get exit door B closed as soon as was possible.

"It's not fair, having to rely on us to do two jobs at once; he's left me right in it" complained Chris.

"You have to think about what mishap he may have had before complaining folks," said Dave. "He could be under a bus for all we know, lads. Then think how you would feel, knowing your friends were complaining. Let's see what's what first."

"Yer, like how many buses run through this stadium each day....?" came a sensible but sarcastic bleat from Bradley.

Drew was not the type of person to be away from duty, it was out of character. Geraldine and Sandi had not been seen around much either. The extra crowd today had brought about a good volume of noise and persons were moving about and it was evident that people were not seen nor heard of as usually would have been.

"All I'm saying is that we should not tar anyone yet," was a final plea from Dave.

"That's all well and good but I say he's done a bunk because he said to me that he would not leave me alone on that mezzanine and he did. Plus the fact that you ought to be looking after them there players right now Dave. I'm a photographer on games not a bleeding removal man," was Chris's own final note.

"You're right mate," said Dave, who promptly dropped his end of the boxed material as they finally got to the large bins near the car park and then marched off to the main entrance.

Bradley did the same.

"Did I have to open my big mouth?" quipped Chris to himself, standing there with mouth open in astonishment. Then tipped what was left of the debris into the bins.

71

Back inside the building owner Mark Atkin was greeting the two statisticians Ronnie and Jim at the new bar in the function room.

"Welcome to the stadium gentlemen. Please have another drink of your choice on me and apologies about the start of the game. Those referees can be a bit fussy from time to time and what can we do about that glass breakage. Tut…These things are set to hold us back but as you can see we are all in order now, driving forward."

He held open his arms as if to show off the function room's splendour. There was a short pause and then he continued. "How are things at your end with affairs as regards the league?" he asked, sipping on his Coke in the interval with Ronnie Nichol and Jim Lydon listening intently.

Jim was first to reply.

"Nice bar you have here in this function room."

With a smile, Mark gleefully credited his staff team and on how they all pulled together to make it work and that the room was the first of a few new ideas for next season.

"Oh thank you, Jim. I have things up my sleeve but you know I can't give away all of my secrets to the opposition owners."

Then let out a large belly laugh before saying," so how are things at HQ."

"Well", added Ronnie. "We also can't disclose all that we know but it's a pity that the rest of your building is not set up as well as this room. The new organisation has good relations with a lot of public sector groups and they want to see rinks made for purpose and that means appealing to the punters. I am afraid you're falling behind others it has to be said. We are here in part as Ice Hockey lovers but - seeing it through the public's eyes - it's failing, Mark. Interested as we are to see the sport flourish, some teams may have to go from the league in exchange for others – get my drift?"

Rather caught out but undeterred Mark responded, "Oh yes dear gentlemen, I do understand and, as we speak, I am revealing a new boot room and skate facility. All mod cons and new seating for a relaxation area, the staff are on it right now as we speak. Did you hear that noise as we came in? It's newly repaired skates being sharpened for re-racking tomorrow."

Mark took another sip from his glass, pleased that he had got out of that one for now. But he was no nearer to finding out what the plans were for the season in money terms. He wanted to know how much and when but they were not giving too much information away at present. He would have to try harder, later.

****

After a talk with the zamboni staff that were parking up and making ready to sweep some left over ice from the corridor, the manager closed up the exit B door behind him and strolled up to the bins in the car park to check on his staff.

"Bradley and Dave have gone missing, Mr.Higson. Left as soon as we dropped the glass here for the bins, they did. Bradley took off towards the gates, mind you, not the main entrance," said Chris Fielding. "Can I go back to the mezzanine as I should? Old Drew is still not around but dare say I'll find him somewhere in the stadium when I get back."

"Yes, yes, go ahead," came the reply. "I'll deal with things regards Bradley but put someone on the lights if Drew is not there. Reginald in the bar or Fred the zamboni driver can help out. I assume Dave has gone to the first aid room, dressing room or such. I was waiting to let you all in as I have asked for all the exits to be fully locked today, a new initiative on security. Oh look - here's Dave wandering back. Probably couldn't get in of course. Let's move on guys, things to do! Come back in via the way we came out."

Tom was not happy and rightly so. It was no better even after the meeting they had gone through earlier with all those warnings. Bradley wherever Bradley was hadn't helped matters. But no one had been informed of the door closures during the game, so no reason for Tom to get so excited about that, but he would do anyway in his anxiousness and agitated state.

Suddenly his phone went off and it was a text from apprentice Andy Gill. He was on the high street opposite Atkins Ltd just 200 yards away next door. Andy Gill had been delivering those letters and forgotten one for 'Marc Twaite's fishing emporium' on Robina Drive, miles away as far as he was concerned.

"Can I do that after the game?" then continued." Just to say I had got back to the office and it was still closed just now as Vicki had taken my key card and locked up. I'd best get back to the stadium and pick one of the other key cards up."

"No, deliver the note…get back to me at the stadium after that." was a rather frantic decision. 'I'll get the matter sorted."

This didn't please Andy; there was a post office just over the road as well. But he wanted to get on with the manager as much as possible even if others didn't. Maybe there would be an opening for him, he thought, if he kept a good record. Though there was little chance of that happening.

All three men marched back to the stadium and were let in by Tom who duly locked up the door again once they were through, then got on his phone again to someone else. Chris ran along the corridor and Dave strutted up after him.

73

Outside, Andy walked along the main street to do as he had been asked to. Then he bumped into the missing Bradley over by the butchers on the other side of the road. Bradley didn't care any more and he was telling Andy this. To the point that he said his "mind had been messed up" and he "wasn't going to let Tom get away with that."

Tom was seething.
"These young uns!" he thought to himself (although he was not that old himself), "it's gone too far this time, I'll get the girls to ring Bradley up and tell him not to come back at all. He's a liability. He's not having this week's wages either; it would cost us more keeping him on. A week in advance notice taken as far as I am concerned".

****

At every opportunity Wayne was going to get 'a piece of the action' so to speak.

He had found out that Maureen Smyth, one of the office gals, had been on a dating site. He usually went on the same one - but not for dating purposes. He more likely saw them as sex opportunities, regularly meeting up with women that turned into one night stands.

This time Maureen, a married woman, was his target and Christmas had come eleven months early as cleaner Sandi, in his own words, was also 'mad for it'. Things were going so well for him that if he had shook a tree; money may as well have dropped out of it.

He was standing by the booking office door after knocking, waiting for Maureen to let him in for an agreed meeting. He must have been mad doing this on game night. The door came ajar.

"Ok you can come in now. But it's a bit tricky as you're supposed to be in the changing room surely…" murmured Maureen as she let him in whilst Elaine was on an errand.

He couldn't wait. Wayne grabbed Maureen round the waist and pulled her close, feeling the rush of excitement knowing they should not be doing this he started to kiss and fondle whatever was at hand. It added to the moment.

She was less enthusiastic but engaged into a long lingering kiss that transformed into clothing being undone and hands slipping underneath. Not as though Maureen had much chance though, it being a one way piece of action. What can you do with a fully geared up hockey player anyway?

This time the unlocked door was pushed opened against Wayne's back and Sandi emerged from the corridor. Maureen gladly sat aside onto a desk near by as the other two, in this threesome, engaged into similar moves, though again it was all Wayne's lead. This time, Sandi was more animated than Maureen's embrace a few seconds previous. Both had been on the same website; both married too, but Sandi less inhibited about it all. If only her husband had known that he had not long ago delivered her to the arms of another.

True to form, time was tight and minutes later Wayne's excuse for more first aid requirement might have been wearing a bit thin with the other players and coach.

This meant he had to get back soon. "I'll see you around, gals" was a promise one of them was looking forward to more than the other.

****

Assuming all had returned to their respective chores.

Geraldine and Sandi would be working on the new skate hire area.

Dave Hallam - yet presently without a first aid room key - would be checking all was ok in there, then be back with Mr.Atkin seated for the second period.

Maureen and Elaine should soon be getting on with duties in the stadium booking office, collating sales.

Andy Gill on his delivery service would be back by next interval.

Should all stewards actually be in place and in blocks, stores, bench or on mezzanine, what could go wrong this period?

Well, Tom was on his way back from the now locked exit/entrance B to ask the girls in the office to make that phone call to Bradley. Then with luck, actually get to see some of the game properly before seeking some solitude over at Akins Ltd next door when taking the profits up to add to the safe at the end of this second period.

"They better had been on the job" he thought and be ready for him. Little did he know how near to that fact he was? Though not ready for him.....

On his 'to do' list Tom had to find a way of getting back into the Atkins building still short of a key card and check upon Andy's troubles before leaving to M A Enterprises. .

Merrivale was bathed in the winter's sunshine. Football results were coming in over from the mid-day matches heard from car radio's as men washed the family car.

"Nottingham Forest 1 Notts County 3….Banbury 1 Oxford 0 and Palompon 2 Giltbrook 0"

Ladies brought in the washing from the garden and prepared for the afternoon tea. Everything was good and hopefully the day would be complete with the 'Mustangs' claiming victory.

Elsewhere, people were back home and relaxing - here - in the posh part of Merrivale close to the lake area. People were enjoying their Saturday afternoon relaxation, considering the weather was very mild.

'Listening to the match on the radio there Bob?'

'Yer, sounds like it's not too bad a game Sid, so I'll drop back in for a cuppa and see what happens'.

'You think it'll be a win for a change?'

'Nah, last time I went it was all over by the first. Used to go a lot as you know but if this new season works out I can give it another go Sid.'

'Yes, a bad season for those Mustangs. But like you I may try and see what's happening if this Cup run goes well'.

Scene Eight
2.04pm   Second Period

"Ok, here we go! Referee Pirry drops the puck and this is the second period!" shouted DJ Dave England who is quick to drop the music from full volume.

The puck hit the ice with a splat and Bob Marshall swept it to Steve Pelletier who was happy to be on the ice and immediately made an impression on the game avoiding all Scorpion checks. But back down to earth the team went as Andy Barton air shots an easy pick up from Steve and slammed his stick onto the ice in frustration because of it. Coach, Chris threw his clipboard onto the floor and got vary animated. As if the team has decided to throw in the towel early, there were yet more mistakes which continued for the next few minutes. Chris ran his hands upwards over his face and then down again showing his annoyance with what was happening. He turned and talked to Steve Butler and then marched off to the dressing room.

Steve took charge of the team lines and, while things didn't improve much more, the score at least stayed the same.

Down in the changing area Chris, after taking one more look outside with the door ajar, lifted out his mobile phone before closing the home team door a little more. He called up a number, and then kept peering out of the room into the corridor in fear of being heard.

"Hello, Chris Phillips here. Trying to get you whilst I can, wondered how things are going?"

The person on the other end had been waiting for this call. It was important to both of them.

"I want this deal sorted here and now." Chris then added, "A good getaway also, it's got to be clean and I don't want any repercussions"

"No fear Chris" a reassuring reply came. "It's sorted; two thousand up front, the rest later as we agreed ok?"..."see you tonight to finalise - Mr. Reynaldo will make contact with you shortly."

The re-opening of the door and Chris's emergence was met with a great cheer by the crowd. Chris tapped Steve on the shoulder once he was back on the bench and Steve leant towards him to give the state of affairs. If he had been frank about it all, the summarising would have gone something along the lines of 'we are shite but 2-0 up guv."

Tom Norton had just sent a sizzling shot from the point, virtually the same position as Molin had scored from but this time the net minder was stood staring ready for this one, yet the speed still beat him anyway.

So, the puck was dropped again by the referee in this period and the contest was at least going ok with regards the score line, even if Mustangs were not firing on all cylinders.

****

'Knock knock'.....

"Hey there, David! Do you hear me?" Dave Hallam shouted as he cracked onto the equipment manager's door. Some seconds later, as time was taken to get to the door with machine sounds stopping abruptly, the door opened.

"You got my key to the first aid room mate? Luckily I haven't had any problems yet with injuries, touch wood, but want to check out the room when I can as someone was in there earlier – shouldn't have passed the key onto you really."

"Sorry, Dave. I have mislaid it as I left my coat over the way but promise I will get back to the Atkin building after doing this skate in 2 minutes if I can. Know where you are so I will get someone to get it over to you, promise."

"OK, dude. It's no rush for now but, in an emergency, I will have to bust the lock and Tom won't be happy with that. I'll end up paying for it and - dare I say - I'll send you the bill" remarked Dave, who hadn't been so stressed during a game for a long while.

"No fear mate, I'm on the job. What's happening in the game? Can't understand what's going on in here" added David.

"Just scored a second and looks good as it's only 5 minutes into the second period."

A rousing cheer went up again from the seating because the scoreboard now showed 3-0 in favour of the home side. Adi Collins – with his 500th career goal - was jubilant jumping from one skate to the other and being mobbed by his line as a loose puck had squirmed from out of the boards' right under his nose and he just flipped it up past a deflated Carlton minder.

The team were not playing well but it transpired that the gods were on their side today. Owner Mark Atkin was up with his hands clapping above his head. Ligaya and Melanei were both hugging each other, because one of their favourite players had got a goal for the team. They would be searching him out after the game again no doubt. In fact looking around the stadium quite a few were doing the same. It was nice to see.

"In fact, make that three nil now," said Dave Hallam as Mr.Temple got back to repairs with a big smile on his face. It was good to be winning and things going the right way for a change.

"GOOOAAAALLLLL, to number #8 Daniel Scott – unassisted!" rang out from Stef on the officials bench as Dee marking the score sheet put a hand on his arm and had a word in his ear…..Adi stopped all celebration and was soon skating up to the officials bench and contested the call. Like Dee he wanted the goal marked down to himself. Bugger playing as a team this was his goal and he was having it.

****

During all this Tom Higson had made his way down the inside corridor to the stadium booking office at the main entrance - which was now closed to the public - with a large card covering the office glass window saying 'closed till game's end'..

Bursting in there he began chatting to Elaine (who was looking all out of breath) and Maureen about money and it certainly looked like a good day as regards income. Sat at their desk the ladies continued to count up the cash flow making a record and putting it into bags ready for Tom to take over to the Atkins office on the main road.

Tom had been asking a series of financial questions and then thought of Bradley.

"Get on the phone to Bradley this instant, Elaine, and inform him that he needs to stay away because any contract with him is terminated forthwith. I'll be sending him a letter detailing his final wages…. Did you lock up and set the exit door alarms as asked?"

"Yes Mr Higson. At the time you had requested but there was a light flashing for exit/entrance B" Elaine replied.

"That was me and the boys going out to the bins, taking some plexi-glass due to health and safety procedures but we're back in now. So it's doing its job then, fine. Just make sure this is not common knowledge at the moment especially with these league officials in today; we'll see how it goes for now. Stops people getting in without payment. As soon as you understand which door has been opened let Chris know on security immediately."

"Oh yes we will and we did" replied Maureen.

Far too many fans had caught onto the idea of crashing into the stadium soon after the puck drop, to avoid paying but security Chris couldn't man every exit. Tom had arranged for the girls to set back into operation the old 'lock down' mechanism which would have all exits simultaneously locked. It was either this for the meantime or more loss on the balance sheet. More effective - Tom thought - yet also an illegal operation due to fire safety regulations and the reason why it was stopped in the first place.

Very soon Tom would be off on another mini complaint because when he and others had exited the door in order to rid the stadium of all the broken glass, security man Chris had not appeared as should have done. He needed to ask why. Telling the ladies he chirped:

"Well, Chris didn't turn up, as I was there. Another little word in an ear is needed once again it seems. This idea won't work if I'm able to get out and back in without him knowing."

Tom, rather disgruntled, exited the office in order to catch some of the game (and hopefully Chris) before his next job which would be to take the money and put it into the safe in the Percy Street office prior to a last journey back to M.A.Enterprises on Port Raven Way.

Elaine was all confused. "Oh blimey, I'm frightened to death. What will he think if I go out and he sees me? He's going to be going over there soon but I need to see Andy who normally goes over with him. Oh blimey, I better get off now" she fretted.

Maureen had not been listening. Since Tom had left she was head down, close to tears and silently fretting herself. She was aware of what Elaine would be on about though uninterested in other people's worries at this moment, she had her own problems.

Elaine repeated that she needed to get out of the building and asked that Maureen cover for her. But Maureen had issues herself and wanted something from Elaine. She knew her friend had a dilemma and needed to get something done but had to get something off her chest.

Sobbing away and very distressed. Maureen confided that she had been on a dating site and behind her husband's back, and had been playing about with another man.

It took some explaining but she had, in fact, met up with Mustangs player Wayne Pitchford and at first, it was a bit of fun. But then Sandi got involved and thinking about it, it was a mistake and a bit too much for her. She had not been so brave before, some of the things that had been going on were making her feel way out of her depth. Sandi was more open to things like that.

"It was not long ago that I was with Sandi and Wayne in the first aid room for an arranged meeting with him for a threesome type of thing then it got a bit out of hand as we met back here after the first period too. I mean you were not here and......well, I wanted something ...er....but this is not it, .it's all going a bit too fast now."

"Bloody hell, Maureen...! Listen - don't worry, I won't say anything. We can work this out together, I won't tell anyone as long as you understand it is very important that you keep Tom in the dark about me and don't say that I have left here again. I must get going, to meet someone near the Atkins office, I have to go. Let me out and back in, turning the system alarm off when I contact you on the phone to get back in and we will sort all this out later for you, babe."

Maureen agreed and with that continued to get the cash bagged up ready for Tom as Elaine left the office. Funnily enough - who did Elaine see first but Sandi making her way over to the new skate hire area, probably off to be doing something like…work!.

Elaine was thinking what a shock it all was but hadn't time to reflect on it. She waited for the door to be let open from the lock mechanism by Maureen.
Then leapt out into the fresh air and ran off in the direction of the boundary railings gate aside the Atkins office building.

****

Arms folded, Tom watched as the Mustangs looked dangerous on the attack and were edging into the Scorpions territory more often but when Carlton counter attacked the home team looking ragged. Carlton were beginning to push forward in search of their first goal nearer the end of the period as Tom's attention began to wander.

Looking around, he could see the seats were taken up more than in previous weeks and this pleased him and, as he scanned around, he saw owner Mark Atkin give him a wave from the other side. This made him think, he ought to get a move on and make this weekend finish on a good note and get that cash put in the safe. Turning back to the main entrance, he had forgotten all about a check on Chris's whereabouts and proceedings as to who was where and were they doing what they ought to be. This would have to wait until later in the day. He could - maybe, drop back here again before going back into Port Raven Way?

Tom was handed the bags of cash by Maureen through the reception window without him seeing that Elaine was missing and he strolled off by himself with a key coded card to Atkins' Ltd firmly grasped in his hand. He had picked this up on his travels from one of his 'trustee' code card holders but he still believed he'd see Andy waiting outside anyway as he had a missed call from him on his mobile, then a text saying 'SEE YA THEN'. Maureen released the door locks once more and nodded as Tom strolled off. Was it to be another threesome, but this time of Tom, Andy and Elaine bumping into each other?

"Ah flip! He's going the way of the side gate." Said Maureen to herself" I hope he doesn't see Elaine over there."

Back around the ice pad, Melanei and Ligaya were out of their seats. Two ear piercing shrills echoed over everything else. The Scorpions Kenny McKie had been on a one-on-one with net minder Neil Edwards. Kenny pulled up short and with Neil still diving in to save the puck with his arm out stretched; a blade caught him on the arm as Kenny's skate tipped up. It looked nasty, but blood on the clear white ice made it worse than it probably was. Yet with a wound dripping blood it wasn't nice to see. Neil immediately skated over to an exit by the boards towards the first aid room area whilst Dave Hallam followed in hot pursuit in a chase around the outside of the playing surface like a greyhound trying as much to get there before him.

Dave looked bemused, Neil was nowhere to be seen down on the corridor level and the first aid room was still locked. Not knowing if this was a good or bad thing he started to run about and asked anyone if they had seen Neil but here on the corridor behind the seating, there were not many people about to ask anyway. He looked one way then the other, no – he wasn't anywhere, odd. Then he checked the changing room. No!
Reserve net minder Killen was in the game now. Taking shots on his pads and into his glove, he looked good practicing for the next, and his, shift. Frankie and the team had to hold out a few more minutes. Going in 3-0 after two periods would be brilliant.

There was nothing to worry about. Play was only halted for the odd discretion or two. It was Bob Marshall who seemed to be tripping to the sin-bin more often than needed, though. Yet Angel held up play as much as needed and Shaun was hitting hard and the clock ticked down to a crowd pleasing chant of '5-4-3-2-1 hurray'.
End of the second period.

Vicki out on the streets looking for someone

Scene Nine
2.42pm   Last Interval/Third Period

The alarm was sounding again to say that a door had been opened. Maureen had to spring into action because Tom had just been on at them about seeing this through. Alerting staff to possible intrusion was not going to be this often was it?

Then again the alarm was saying that it was the main entrance just beside the booking office, so she might as well have a look herself, seeing as Chris had not turned up last time.

Opening the office door and leaning out to surmise what was going on, she immediately saw that glass was on the floor and the door itself was broken in part and, to add, blood was dripping from a single pane of glass and the handle. No one was about apart from people starting to clamber down from the stairways at ice level towards her.

Looking around not many people were there in the corridor. She looked left and there were some guys approaching but none walking away, as if they had come in. Then again, it was too hard to tell now as folk mingled about and it got far worse to worry about.

Looking down the corridor past the first aid and function room, all that could be seen was the figure of Dave Hallam and he didn't seem too bothered about anything. More figures jumped down from the stairs around him and past into the function room for a drink at the bar or others swiftly manoeuvred to the toilet areas within.

Maureen eyed the situation up and then decided to stick a caution notice to a chair against the door after turning the alarm off inside the office. She then alerted Sandi to 'get this cleaned up please' who immediately said she'd 'get Geraldine on the job'.

True to Sandi's words, Geraldine trooped up with bucket and cloth and suitably attired with personal protective equipment. She then tried to wipe the area free of fluid or any sharp glass that lay around.

Back by exit/entrance C, Chris Fielding was speaking with Drew as others filed past chatting about the game excitedly.

"You're going to be in big trouble mate' said Chris. 'Tom's after your skin."

Looking unworried glaring back at Chris he replied "Well he'll find trouble himself doing that at the moment."

"What do you mean by that, then" was the obvious query.
"No matter ...nothing." Then Drew just walked off in the direction of the entrance where he could see Geraldine by the door sweeping up and then he looked at his watch which read 2.55pm before walking away.

Suddenly, Andy Gill came running in past through the open door, walking all over some glass and brushing against the door itself. Ignoring Geraldine at his feet, he started to run off between people in the direction of the changing rooms then changed his mind and switched route to the stairs on his left in order to go up to ice level. An open hand pressed against his chest and held him back. It was Chris Whittaker who pushed Andy an inch or two asking. "What's all the rush? Something to run away from, or is it to?"

"No nothing – truth." Said a very anxious and perspiring young man, then in a panic ran off up the stairs and began looking around quickly before disappearing into the seated area.

****

3.10pm
The players were on the way out for the last period. Fans returned to their seats in great anticipation and DJ Dave England made some announcements about next weeks match at home and then blew the roof with a tune that was followed by a jingle ending in a heartbeat pounding to raise the atmosphere.

With a confidence not seen thus far this season, the Mustangs skated around like they were hot property for any scout that may be on the look out for new talent. The referee blew his whistle and the sides lined up against each other for the last twenty minutes of play. The crowd was hyped; players were ready, the officials too.

The puck was dropped by referee Gordon Pirry for the last session.

It covered all of the ice for the next ten minutes. Play switched from defence to attack, bodies swapped checks upon each other, grabbing and clutching ensued. But no one got near the opposition's goalie.

Fans sat to the edge of their seats. It seemed to be a new and better Mustangs team thus far. The town had not seen such a good performance in ages. If they could stay together as a team, maybe everyone on and off the ice would gel together as a unit and things would improve.

However the tank may just be going into empty as mistakes started to crop up. The team were on the back foot, skating backwards far too often into a defensive game. The coach started to pace up and down and players were changing far more often wanting a rest. In a matter of 10 minutes from the start the advantage had turned to Scorpions.

Individual flair showed at times yet the clock wasn't ticking down fast enough for the home fans as they also realised that they were in trouble. Then again they could rely on a time out which would rejuvenate the side into a last 10 minute spurt surely considering the home advantage along with good luck, endeavour and …good luck again.

But the coach and players started to look glum on the benches as things turned around to the Scorpions' advantage by this 50th minute and suddenly backs were against the wall.

Adi Collins was dropped into defence to help out and, with Bob Marshall and Andy Barton seemingly getting tired (as they slipped and tripped around the ice), they let the Scorpion offence through far too many times. Andy at one point almost bent over the boards as if given up and not wanting to either climb over or move away from it due to exhaustion.

"' Come on guys - muscle up! Skate or get off the ice" shouted Steve Pelletier who was itching to get back on himself.

Most players looked across at Coach Chris waiting on eye contact in order to get the go ahead to get back into the fray; however, not all were so keen. Wayne was done, maybe all the frolics from before had not helped. Even Paul was getting less pumped to the latter stages of the game.

Gary Stefan rallied the troops after a time-out called by the coach who was asking for more. Then Chris started getting angry at individuals, as it was becoming desperate.

17.15 into the third or with 2.45 left in the game – which ever way you wanted to look at it – Scorpions did what everyone would have put money on. They scored against Killen who was left out to dry, stranded by the defence. But the puck went through his legs as he tried to kick it away on a straddle in front of net. Some could blame him and some definitely would, but the question for now was 'would the team hold out?' …It was now 3-1.

Suddenly Vicki burst into the stadium through the broken entry door clipping the chair with the sign on....she stood there holding up her hand and looked around as if she'd expect to see someone in front of her but then checked left and saw Maureen within the booking office and waved at her as if it was an important issue to be dealt with.

'Hi, it's me. Get yourself over here I have some good news.'

'Oh blimey am I glad to see you.'

What looked like Bradley, wandering about the street over the road!

Scene Ten
3.48pm

End of game

Antoine was doing a perfect job. This would be an upset for equipment manager David Temple as - even though he didn't want things to mess up - it could be disastrous if Antoine was given the job outright. After all, the day was going well: a big crowd, good score line and looking like a win and two points.

But now Antoine was off running to fetch hockey sticks as both Steve Butler and Tom Norton had clashed and both of theirs had broken, which just added to the bad luck they had been having over the last few minutes.

He ran down the stairs between the seating and then jumped onto corridor level, spotting the managers wife, Vicki, who was just going into the booking office!

He ran down to the equipment area. At the same time the door to the equipment/technicians room (next to the first aid room) swung open. David Temple starred straight into Antoine's eyes as he ran past but, to avoid conflict, Antoine lowered his gaze then noticed a wound on one of David's hands. Cut from the chore of skate sharpening he guessed. But he did not want to talk to David and so carried on in a hurry to get those sticks.

The scoreboard was clinging onto 3-1 as the Scorpions pelted rubber after rubber against leg, stick and pads. They must have been a little aggrieved, not only because this was not materialising into a second goal and the possibility of an extra attacker for the equaliser but because they had taken an early hit from the Mustangs' good play in this game. They would be kicking themselves for letting the lower ranked team in - dip in play of recent or not - such was the competitive nature of the team.

The best thing of all for Merrivale was the fact that, play aside, the dreaded one goal loss was not going to be a point of tomorrow's newspaper article. Mick Holland would have to dream up a new heading as the clock again ticked down the last 30 seconds, without a glimmer of a chance of removing the net minder by Carlton. Perhaps they thought the goal difference was best left that way considering the handicapped point system.

The buzzer sounded at 3.45pm to rapturous applause from all around the stadium. Both Melanei and Ligaya rushed off to the side of the block they were in, to seek out the eye candy and amidst all the furore, Jona and Richard were off towards the changing room to try and catch a picture or quote for the fanzine.

What a match! There were great smiles on everyone's faces as the Mustangs wheeled around the ice after the hand shakes with the opposition, to take stance for the presentations. No 'Man of the Match awards here, just a gift of a crate of ale from the local 'Caveman's' public house over the road.

A stream of fans then started to manoeuvre away towards the exits which, of course, had been switched to 'open' by Maureen ever since the breakage of the main door with glass which had strewn all over.

Delayed players trotted down into the dressing rooms and supporters cheered them on. Even Elaine was back from her exploits over the way towards town. She could now relax and her face lit up as soon as she got back into the booking office, seeing Vicki there with Maureen, Elaine got some good news after all her earlier worries.

4pm and the place was near empty.

****

Dave England was starting to pack up as the last of the fans were leaving the building. Chris on security duties was walking around the building shutting the exits.

"It's been a good day today, don't you think? Said Dave

"Sure has, I've cleaned up today with some overdue matter and I'm off over the road for a jar or two. Are you coming along?" said Chris - which Dave had to decline due to him having to attend a function.

"I'll tell you what, though. If we keep playing like that we'll end up getting something from this season," chipped in Dave again.

"I'll tell you something too, Dave. You get some more tunes going on a match day and we'll all be happy – keep playing that Gary Glitter any more and I'll put in a request for a new DJ. "

Walking past at that moment was Tony Grainger who came upon the two of them unwittingly. Looking a bit startled, he ignored Chris and said "see you later, Dave." To which Dave mirrored the quote.

Chris then added "Don't mind me TG! You just pop along and stick to your own side of the building next week."

Tony ignored this. He wanted to turn round and say something back but felt uneasy in this situation and knew he could always get his own back later.

Tony walked on and heard a laugh echoing in the near empty building and he took a kick at the chair still sitting by the broken door which slid into the wall. A few pieces of glass once again hit the floor.

Coming from the new skate hire facility, Sandi was just a few paces behind him. "Hey, I've got someone coming in to sort this out, no need for you to make it any worse."

Tony just grunted and made his way off over the car park.

'Ohh, I can't stand that guy. He just makes me mad. I'm going to get even once and for all. But the trouble is he's got that power of influence but I know for sure I can sort this out once and for all. The bigger they are the bigger they fall'.

At this time of day the light was still good outside though shadows were long gone by now.

****

Twenty minutes later players started to emerge from the changing rooms and went their own way. Some went out via the back entrance and others were picked up at the front. It was still early afternoon so the light was good but chilly. Virtually last out and making his way over to see Tom in the Atkins building next door was the coach. He left behind him a long faced Sandi who was staying on with Geraldine to see that the door was sorted as well as getting the facility cleared up ready for tomorrow. It had been a long day already.

Chris Phillips had things on his mind and paced over to the boundary fence, mulling over the game and thinking about how the owner would be relieved with the result.

He pushed open the gate to the side of Atkins'. Closed it again behind him and turned onto the main street where the front entrance awaited him. The door was ajar; he did not have to knock at all. All was quiet but for the noise of a murmur upstairs - void of Tom's usual ranting or moaning. Chris got to the top step and called out but no one answered. But he could see that the door at the end of the corridor was open a little, as some light was showing through from the windows - and no one was in the main office that overlooked Lord Percy Street.

He walked along the corridor and passed by the meeting room and the store room and then things became a bit clearer as to why he had heard no answer seconds ago. Two black suited legs could be seen lying flat and lifeless on the floor, Chris was now a bit cautious. He moved ever closer to the coaching room and saw that it was not just one person that was there but two - as he saw a moving shadow thrown by a light that was on.

Chris slowly turned the corner at the door as a 'click' from the camera behind went off.

The body of Tom Higson, was face down pointing towards the back of the room, motionless. Young Andy Gill was sitting at Tom's head with his hands dripping of blood.

Chris could see that Tom had a gaping wound on his head.
Andy – fearful of what had happened – slowly looked up at Chris and muttered...

"He's dead."

At Police Headquarters, Inspector Iain Dilley gets a phone call

'Hello Sir, I'm so sorry to disturb you. There is a call on line seven.'

'OK, Cynthia I'll take it'.

'Hello, Inspector Dilley here, Merrivale chief police offices.....ahem.....ahem....yes....

Alright, I'll be straight on to it. You say the stadium on Lord Percy Street. Right I'm on my way.'

'Not till after this nice piece of fruit cake though.'

Getting on the phone himself...

'Thomas, get your coat and the team out, we are off to Percy Street. I've got something important to finish at the moment so meet me at the car downstairs in five.'

The receptionist intervened.

'Call on line three Sir, its Mrs Dilley.'

'Oh, tell her you missed me Cynthia, I'm out of the office.'

'See you later cake.'

Scene Eleven
5pm

Police Interviews

The usual had happened. Word had got around that there had been a major incident over at Atkin's Limited. The stadium was still open with a few personnel completing the close down of operations. But the gates wouldn't be locked up just yet as more official cars drove into the front of the blue building. Most of them were police that were making sure that whoever didn't need to leave stayed put and those that were not needed, were sent on their way.

The main entry point was guarded by constables as others were rounding up persons from inside the stadium in order to start interviews and ascertain a position of control.

All supporters had gone bar a few that had stayed on just outside the gates to see what it was all about. Rumours suggested that someone had been killed at the complex next to the Mustangs home. Surely there has to be a connection?

Coach Chris and apprentice Andy were retained in the upstairs office for further questioning, Andy was quivering with fear and frightened as to what may happen to him.

Chris had called the authorities in and it was a very quick response. The environment was secure and the most important two of the investigating troops were stepping out of their cars, having driven straight up to the stadium main door. One got out and went round to the other side of the car to join the man in charge. It was Sergeant Neil Thomas with Inspector Iain Dilley.

Dilley had already set things in motion and officers had been given orders to glean whatever they could from around the vicinity. Certain individuals were assigned specifics but he wanted to start from where the foul play had occurred and thus marched straight over to the boundary gates and through them to Atkin's front door where the area had been taped off, closely followed by Sergeant Thomas.

They met up with forensics already there and were updated to affairs then Dilley wasted no time in telling all that the incident had been witnessed. A worker over at the next office block at Chambers Logistics had been looking out of her window and saw two people in a tussle. So the Inspector wanted nothing but true facts from Chris and Andy as to what each were doing in the building, when they had come in, what for and for how long.

"I can now understand why you were so quick to get here Sir, after my call to you. I found young Andy here in this state kneeling over the body when I came in after the match at the stadium." said Chris.

After quizzing more about what each had been doing there and to where they had been on the top floor, the Inspector turned to Andy and asked a series of questions. Andy was rapid in speech and still very nervous; agitated only by the fact that Chris was glaring at him all the time.

He told the Inspector,

"I was out delivering things to people and then couldn't get back in because she had the key code, though it was mine and I should have had it and...."

"Slow down, boy, and just tell me who you're talking about," was Iain Dilley's request.

"OK, I lent my key code that lets you in downstairs, to the secretary. Her name is Vicki. Then I left to deliver letters, Tom - who's in there - told me to just finish my job and then I was supposed to meet him later as usual to let him back in here. But I had no key so I got here and couldn't see him so I looked for him at the stadium but couldn't find him there either, so I came over here again and saw the door open. Came in and there he was. So I tried to help him wake up. You see - I got a call from him saying to help him as he was here. That's when I was over here, ya see."

Inspector Dilley probably understood most of the rambling response and suggested he'd catch up with him later. For now, he wanted forensics to do a check regards the blood over Andy and to do the usual crime scene checks. By now this coaching room and the whole stadium were cordoned off and the inspector was going to get down to what this was all about.

First of all, Chris explained the position with regard the key codes and who had one.

Pointing across to Andy he listed…"Andy Gill, equipment technician David Temple, the security man Chris Whittaker and me, Sir."

The Inspector took a deep breath before stating.

"So you and these guys will be major suspects until proven different. Please listen to my fellow officers and we'll get down to what happened believe me. I'm not stupid to think that other people can't obviously be involved, please let me do my job and abstain from any travels from Merrivale for now.

This is Sergeant Thomas who will be working alongside me throughout. He will take you aside and interview you further. I will speak more with Andy."

****

It was soon realised that owner Mark Atkin was not available, away somewhere, but Iain Dilley wanted him found and delegated (as usual) the chasing task to his side kick Thomas. The technicians - if not found in the building - were rounded up and brought back to Merrivale's main Police headquarters to make it easier to gather information. Once they were furnished with more of the story, they could start to release the people who were obviously free of guilt. But, for now, it was vital to get tough on folk and get facts as early as possible.

The next to be spoken to was Steward Tony Grainger who had left the site in a temper when security man Chris had yet again been teasing him. He told the Inspector how Chris had been seen around the main entrance at the time the murder had happened - which would have been after the second period and before Tom was found after the game. The facts accrued by the police department narrowed the crime down to this exact period but were not announcing this to anyone as yet. The body was being examined by a coroner and the time of death was an important issue as regards people's whereabouts. But proof of who had time and ability to be there at around this period needed to be set in stone. Tony went into detail as to him seeing Chris leave the main entrance - looking sheepishly - and carrying what looked like a knife with him.

He continued:

"Oh yes, and when down by rink side he was talking to player Paul Hacking and they were talking about killing someone. Obviously it would not be Paul as he was playing but as Mr. Tom Higson has been found dead it has to be those two involved."

No one would be left out in the efforts to catch the criminal. Office staff member Maureen had admitted to having been suspiciously in places where she should not have been. This would be the tale of many individuals throughout the investigation and working out if it measured towards them being innocent or an accomplice or may have even dealt the criminal act.

Wayne got wind of the news that he might get caught out as regards his movements within the stadium. He had a dilemma as to what he could say without telling lies yet also not getting himself in further trouble with regards to his assignations with two ladies – and goodness knows what more. He was rather concerned of what the next few days might bring – and he wasn't the only one, for sure.

Several hours later, the police were now focusing on the crimes findings and other organisations started to get their acts together.

The local radio station reported the news of a dead body being found on the main High Street. For the next few days, the newspaper columns would unfortunately not be headlining how the Mustangs fortunes had turned and that the 3-1 home win meant they were in a position to pursue the next round in the Davis competition.

Instead, the murky murder of that day would overshadow the good news and the headlines would read 'MUSTANGS MANAGER MURDER MAYHEM'.

****

The next day the two police officers were back at the station and taking further interviews with those they thought could help with proceedings.

David Temple was seated in front of them and being asked questions about work colleagues, the stadium and the ethics of a days work. He was asked a series of questions that caused him to lower his brow as if to show uncertainty as to why he was being asked these.

"I was sharpening skates as I had been asked to. Then I had to drop over to the office to leave a package for Tom. But that was far earlier then when you're talking about - him being over there. Just ask Drew and Geraldine who I spoke to. Tom would go and take the takings to the safe at the end of the second period every game. I went over before then.

Later about that time he came and knocked on my door where I was and asked to borrow my key code to get in. He said something about Andy not being there and no trust in anyone else as they were missing all the time. Security Chris Whittaker was one such person he said, so needed mine to get into the Atkin office. What can I say other than that. The reason I had the first aid key was because I had cut my hand early on and went to see if I could get a bandage – I got the key to there from Mr.Hallam. I also borrowed this key to player Wayne so he could get a finger guard and because I hadn't got it back, admit I lied to Dave about it being in my coat at the office because I felt bad".

Even fans Jona and Richard did not escape the policemen's attention. They had spoken to the papers about what they 'thought' had happened. Jona had been taking photos whilst at the match and, afterwards, had been by the dressing rooms snapping away.

She told the press that she had good pictures that may help. She obviously made sure that a sum was paid for them to be assured of a nice 'earner' to begin the new fanzine. But this would have to be used later when the newspaper wanted it as another exclusive scoop. The picture emblazoned on their front page at the moment was of Paul Hacking and Vicki after the match swapping money for something and it was just opposite the front door to the stadium. For some reason, the newspaper seemed to think this picture would go well as a follow up from a few weeks before, when it was disclosed that money was a problem at the club. However, Mick Holland's most recent jibe was that the owner was not so handy at using it for the right purposes and seeing Paul and Vicki in the vicinity of the murder zone with cash in hand played into theirs for a good story.

"I'm trying to deal with a very difficult situation here, lady. I gather that you'd not want to be involved too much as regards obstructing the course of my enquiries," said the Inspector.

Jona apologised and then blamed Richard who had urged her to 'make some money' from the opportunity.

"But I heard 'Dead right, going to make a killing' at the Caveman's pub before the game" she replied in her defence.

"I'm not considering you as being involved in this, of course. But maybe I could take a look at all of your pictures from that evening...? That would be considered as helping me with my investigation. You can also tell that to your friend Richard".

What made things worse was that Tony Grainger had also 'spilled the beans' with the paper and after speaking with the Inspector had embroiled into letting them know of the ' I'll kill him' comment which Tony had told the officers about, that happened at ice level between Paul and Chris by the boards. This was even worse for the police as it was also getting in the way of proceedings......

With the lesser of fry leaving the Police station, Inspector Iain Dilley turned to more important matters. He made a phone call to ask about Bradley Brooks and his disappearance that afternoon.

"I'm fed up of being told what to do. He gets on my nerves and that's what I'll tell him when I see him" said Bradley.

"Well how are you going to do that, Bradley? I assume you're up to date with things around town, my lad"? Iain replied.

"What are you on about? I told your other guy that I'm in Coventry and have been since yesterday afternoon. I left work and for the last time. I did a job on some broken glass then buggered off. You can ask Tom, Andy or any of those misfits at Mustangs."

"So, you're telling me that you're not in Merrivale now and have not been since....? Ok, listen - make sure you are on hand for my sergeant to speak with you if need be, Bradley, or there'll be trouble. Just be on this phone number for the next 24 hours. Other than that, I'm happy with what you say. Go missing and I'll have a warrant for your arrest."

The phones went down. Bradley elected not to ask any questions. He had no intention of messing around with the police - enough is enough.

Dilley made a quick call to Sergeant Thomas....." Neil, check out the whereabouts of Bradley Brooks since yesterday, will you? I am keen to know if he's playing games with me. "

****

Another policeman knocked at the door and came in. "It's a Mr. Andrew Blatherwick and Mrs Geraldine Ellis - outside Sir."

"Brilliant, come in - come in – take a seat......Now then, Andrew. Have you got something to tell me?"

The day is going to be a long one for everyone concerned. Geraldine's knees were knocking, anticipating the interrogation. What had they found out, had Drew and she got their stories right?

The Sunday

Sunday, January 24th, 2021

Mustangs Murder Mayhem

Exclusive news within our Sunday issue today. Mick Holland exposes revelation of a shocking murder at the Ice Hockey Atkin building. Post game yesterday Mustang Ice Hockey general manager Tom Higson was found dead in the adjoining office to the stadium on the high street. This follows news that the club was in financial difficulties. Our picture within the 'Whatever' section of today's paper shows

Mustang's own tough guy Paul Hacking in secretive meeting with the murdered victim's wife Jacki Higson, outside the stadium, exchanging a package of money. 'Ill gotten gains' or payment? Read more inside, page 32 with comments from fans Ligaya Damayo, Melanei Wagman, upcoming fanzine contributors Jona Dolores and Richard Archer plus club worker Tony Granger.

Rer
foll
imp

The
that
rela
the
beh
of a
exp
in l
its
beh
con
or v

Scene Twelve
Monday

Further Investigations

The Forensic laboratory had sent back the test results. Sergeant Thomas was collating over blood samples from both body and materials.

He'd also been viewing CCTV and photographs taken at the ice hockey event the previous day.

He was also keenly interested in the security camera set-up within Atkins' Limited in the upstairs corridor, especially as they seemed to be missing timings. For some reason they were also undated.

Meanwhile, the inspector was out and about in the local community. Funnily enough, bumping into Paul Hacking who was taking in a local charity cricket match played this wintry Sunday!!

"Surprised to see you here Paul, I thought you might be putting your feet up today. This looks a little sedate for you - believed you to be all for the hustle and bustle of a fast paced game. Maybe I've got you wrong…?" was Dilley's opening comment.

"Well, don't judge a book by its cover. I'm open to anything. Why don't you just give people a rest, mate?" replied Paul. "You spoke to most of us yesterday and I told you everything I know. I was on the ice all the game, you know that. Unless you think I'm part of some conspiracy then you need to give me some space."

"The trouble is - you didn't like Tom. You're seeing his wife and all you guys have connections, so everyone's under suspension in this close - knit group under one roof. But if you think you need the space, I'll call on you later. Just don't go on your travels anywhere just yet. There's a lot to be done in the next couple of days. I've heard you and Vicki have got itchy feet…. I'll be seeing you later..." were Dilley's final comments.

It was not long before he met up with Chris Whittaker by the lake. This time it was an arranged meeting. The inspector went straight to the point asking.

"Why did you say 'I'll kill him? And "what's the interest in exit door A? The Inspector had plenty more questions too, they came thick and fast.

"You seemed to be missing a lot of the time during the match on Saturday when people were looking for you. Plus you have a good relationship with Paul I hear but he isn't coming up with anything concrete for me as yet – maybe you're more willing to give me your account? "

Chris began to confide in some detail something that was going to fill in a few holes of the investigation. Seemed the Sunday stroll was going to be productive after all. The two continued to walk and lament over the past and, in particular, the last forty eight hours.

Chris threw in a few additional explanations to what he had already given the inspector in the last fifteen minutes or so. The puzzle was being pieced together.

"He (meaning Steward Tony Grainger) never liked me; he's just saying any old rubbish to get at me. Where was he all night? Not in block 3 where he should have been. I'll tell you this…"

But at this moment the inspector had heard plenty and interrupted, calling time on the conversation. He had enough of the entire 'blame others' scenario. For now he had to be on his way and speak to one more soul who he thought was a big part of this jigsaw.

This time sat in - 'Mustangs number one drink station' - 'Mary's Café' he was staring straight into the eyes of Vicki Higson (née Wright). She was lavished in make-up as usual - even at this sombre time.

"Listen, I was not there when all this was happening. I wasn't feeling too well earlier on and that's why I left Atkins'. I took Andy's key card and code so I could lock up and rang Elaine to ask if she would meet me on her way in to work. She was going to give it back to Andy for me but also worried that Tom might tell her off because she'd not be working. Trouble is she never got to hand the key over. Sacrificed half the game too trying to get it all sorted." said Vicki.

"I know"

"How"

"No worries, I just do. Glad you've confirmed my suspicions. I know you didn't kill Tom but you have to tell me more."

Another cup of tea and a few tears from Vicki elapsed before both were satisfied and they eventually bade farewell.

Cricket in winter?

The Lake's Lodge close to where the Inspector met Chris Whittaker

With a murderer on the loose, this last weekend seemed very quite. No movement by the railway with people coming in. It was noticed that people were moving out of the Travel lodge though.

Scene Thirteen
Thursday   The Funeral

It was the day of the funeral. Some of the stadiums working staff were there, to the surprise of the Inspector.

Mind, he was trying to catch up on a few things and to be able to speak to them now was an advantage. He saw Geraldine with her head bowed. Maybe to keep hidden and avoid Dilley but, then again, she may just have been feeling bad about how she had treated Tom. Maybe she had no real axe to grind, just took advantage of circumstances. Funny how things turn out!

The other three characters of Sandi, Maureen and Elaine stood together elsewhere by the grass verge a little further away from the actual grave. Given that they were standing away from the service, Iain Dilley took the opportunity to say hello.

Elaine acknowledged him and said in conversation "I text Andy, you know. Because he text me earlier to say he hadn't got his key. I knew this as I was doing a favour for Vicki who called me before the match. But the lad wasn't there when I left the stadium to look out for him. So I don't know how he got into the building."

"I realise he was found with the body," she continued," but I don't think he has the nerve to do something like that. I had given up waiting so left to go back to the stadium."

"I never saw Tom at all," she went on, "but everyone said that he was coming over to the Atkin office when I was over that way. I didn't do anything but look out for Andy then got back so as to help Maureen. She did me a favour working on her own a while, I should have been there in the office."

Iain just smiled and then heard from Maureen who agreed with what Elaine had said.

"I can tell you that when I looked out after the door's glass was broken, I saw something." said Maureen.

"I thought I'd seen someone by the bins but never thought anything of it. Only looked out for whoever was around the stadium area. Whoever was by the bins could not have been the one breaking out because I got to the door in ten seconds and no one could have got to the bins in that time." She added.

"Or break in…" was a short and only reply from the Inspector.

The ceremony had been quick with no real family members attending for Tom other than a brother. The funeral went as well as any other. Looking around at the people that had come, Dilley was unsure who was who. There were very few that he recognised but colleague, Sergeant Thomas, pointed out the Mustangs' number one net minder. Why was he here?

"I felt as though I should be here" said Neil. "Not many got on with him but I thought you'd be here and wanted to talk to you at some stage - not in the church but maybe afterwards."

"I'm glad you came over, he continued, "Because I wanted to say that when I left the ice I was taking a short cut to get my hand sorted. I had a cut from the clash in the game. I had a few things on my mind and didn't go to the changing room straight away as I'd left my pads and stuff in the crease. But while I was on my way into the corridor, I heard a door's glass break and I back-tracked to see what was wrong. I hid behind a pillar and heard footsteps running in but I saw no one till Maureen came out of the booking Office. I then moved on. Left my other kit in the changing room later and just went home and got the hand sorted because I knew it wasn't life threatening."

Iain looked Neil up and down and gave nothing away when he responded.

"My job entails upsetting a lot of people even if they are seemingly happy to help me. Some try to hide facts yet give away far too much information without knowing it. In a way I'm shuffling a pack of cards and eliminating folk. Why you didn't see the first aid guy I don't know for sure but for some reason you feel as though you had to say this. I can't say anything in return at present but soon I will want to see everyone again at some stage and I think I'll speak to all at the same time back at the stadium which is more convenient. We will get the chance to talk before then in private - don't you worry."

Not knowing what he might have done - put his foot in it or anything - Neil left after the funeral looking as gloomy about things as he always did.

On the way from the church, Inspector Ian Dilley made his way back to the main road and caught up with young Andy Gill, who was walking on his own.

He wasn't sure if Andy had actually been to the funeral or not so he put his hand onto his shoulder and just reminded him not to go anywhere as he'd still need to summarise things. Immediately Andy wanted to reassure that he had nothing to do with the whole mess. Dilley told him not to worry.

"Before 2 o clock I rang the manager to say that I had not got the key card. I then went to the match after I texted Elaine, I know because I checked my watch." Andy volunteered.

"She didn't answer me but she was around there I've been told, so she has done the murder. I went to the stadium to look for Tom because he didn't answer his phone. But he did later. I went back to the Atkin office because I couldn't find him and then there he was on the floor in the coaching room. I bet she was trying to steal the money he took over there." he quickly added.

"Ok. Thank you for that, Andy. Stop worrying! Just tell the truth and anytime you want to speak you can also see Sergeant Thomas at the station." Ian replied.

"Everyone had now left the burial ground bar two grounds men laying Tom to rest".

Scene Fourteen   Summing Up

Dilley and Thomas were booked in for a meal at 'The Bunkers Hill public house'.
This is where all of Sergeant Thomas's work came to fruition, it helped explain a few
things and discard reason to chase up other leads. It all came down to photographs
once again. Not just the ones taken by Chris Fielding that had been confiscated but the
ones that the Atkins building camera took when people entered the coaching room.
Thomas explained that the mechanism that operated the taking of pictures had been
tampered with and the photos seemed to be a bit non specific at first.

"Then I started to lay out the pictures along with our photographic department, Sir!"
Thomas excitedly described.

"The timings of the photos – which were usually shown on the images - had been
deliberately removed - or perhaps it was never switched on in the first place. But what
would the point be of not using that option it it's supposed to be a security system?"

"Indeed" said the Inspector. "Just match them up and be sure that some clever
character didn't walk in backwards or something, in order to fool us. It's bad enough
that the dates and times are missing. That just throws another spanner in the works for
us. It may just be that the machine was faulty but we need to check that. You'll need
to follow that one up."

Thomas continued. "OK but, assuming that it had been someone who had a key card
to get in; perhaps they would also need to have the knowledge to be able to
manipulate this TV camera prior to the murder. Had they the time to do this?

Now as regards Tony Grainger it appears that he and Chris, the security chap have
had a long standing hatred for each other.

Some of the things said by Tony about Chris don't stand up. It's obvious they have
merely had vendettas.

We'll have to slap some kind of action on one or both if they are causing us more
work, Guv - getting in the way of things.

Just to say also, that all these folk who suggest that other people had cut hands is
causing confusion .There was so much happening at the same time, although I
understand that we can't just eliminate them all until we have things confirmed.
Antoine suggests the equipment manager had a cut hand from skate sharpening and
saw him after he appeared from his room trying to hide it. However, Temple
borrowed a key from Hallam saying he had a cut from work but that was ages before
Antoine noticed the cut nearer the end of the game. These are two more gentlemen
who are at odds with each other, Boss."

"Yes," replied Dilley, "as you also related to me earlier, Thomas. Dave Hallam insists
that his first aid room key was borrowed and then, perhaps, used in some form to hide
people away before venturing outside as this room is near an exit.

But I agree with you.
It was taken by Temple in order to help his friend and Mustang player Wayne use the first aid room for – ahem - personal reasons. Maureen has wilted and confided in the fact that she and Sandi the cleaner were party to some, shall we say, interests of their own. We will have to discuss that one another day. Was this first aid key re-used for other purposes?

Chris Phillips has even said that Tom put pressures upon him…as everyone else.

Now, to the real matter we are involved in here. Who murdered Tom Higson? I have whittled the possibilities down to one or two in particular. See if you agree."

The two ordered another coffee and entered into more discussion such as:

"Andy could have returned to say he found the body but stayed with him. Never left the building once he had entered - that's for sure according to the Chambers office staff over the way. Apparently did not search or touch Tom apart from shaking him so much that he got blood all over himself. Then we arrived and found not one but two key cards on the body and a mobile in Tom's hand."

"I still can't grasp why net man Edwards didn't take action to see to his injury – and why he didn't go to the first aid room? Or was that still locked? But not to go to the changing room where Dave Hallam went looking for him, suspicious as he said he did not leave the stadium initially. But the photos we have did then explain something away on that one, though they are grainy and need blowing up still."

"David Temple and this first aid room palaver. A key causing people not to go there for treatment, or is this just some excuse? Truth is Dave Temple may have given the key to that first aid room to someone, but at what time and for how long?"

Then the inspector said, "Thomas, I want you to go on a run for me. Get yourself down to the stadium. Then run over to Atkins, into the building and back again. Tell me how you got on and don't forget to time yourself. "

After Thomas made his energetic run for his superior he took time out to check on the local Emporium to confirm his suspicions of something.

The Inspector wasn't finished there. He went off to investigate some more - particularly regarding the key cards and code and why Tom had two of them. He drove up to the police station and asked for extra finger print specialist results that he would scrutinise. All the blood tests had been done using the local hospital facilities; he had to get confirmation to prove that his suspect was not going to get away with this on some technicality.

This was an odd case because of the extreme circumstances of foul play that could have come from so many people and the fact that there was a diverse range of odd things happening in that one period of time centered on the game's second period and the subsequent period break.

Tom had left the stadium by himself. Some people could be accounted for as out of the stadium at this time but others, who were within the stadium, could be guilty of the crime by measure of being an accomplice!

Back in his office, he drew a sigh of relief after some thought. He knew that he had just a few things to tie up before he'd be having a group talk with all of the workers the next day. What better place to talk with all but back at the stadium tomorrow and reveal some interesting but disturbing news to them also?

He grabbed the phone from off his desk, lent forward on both elbows and dialled a number he knew very well.

"Thomas? Yes, mate. Go and arrest Chris Whittaker and net minder Neil Edwards as we had agreed upon....right now."

The hospital was very helpful with their laboratories

Scene Fifteen
Saturday   'Who did it?'

It was the morning of the meeting and all was quiet around the stadium. Not only the rink itself - but the whole atmosphere outside too, it was both gloomy and eerie. The workers who were to be addressed were as glum as well as mournful. It might as well have been the funeral all over again as they mingled in patches around the function room.

The Inspector and Sergeant walked in and invited all to sit down. Then took hold of paperwork and sat at pre arranged tables facing everyone. It looked more like a post murder TV appeal to the press rather than a general meeting of all that had worked there; those that Dilley and Thomas wanted to see were now seated ahead of them. Some would hear shocking news, others would be relieved. However, they were all to get bad news concerning their futures.

Some individuals would still have to be cleared of certain allegations against them, more so because of what they had been involved in at the stadium rather than being the object of murder, so quite a few were apprehensive.

Inspector Dilley stood up.

'Well, hello all, I can tell you that I have everything in hand and am now able to state a few findings. Some individuals are not with us because they are being dealt with at this very moment for unlawful practices. You are here because I want to be able to make clear our findings. To tell you the truth"....and as he peered over his reading glasses to them "nothing but the truth. So you can forget all that you have heard, read or reckon to have known".

He started to pace up and down in front of Sergeant Thomas and two uniformed officers.

"I've never been to investigate something before that has had me witnessing so much turmoil in one place. Not solely because of this crime but the people who work here having so much hatred, vendetta and mischievousness. You seem to delight in each other's downfall, whilst making the most for yourselves. But all this is about to end."

Walking ever closer to those nearest him he lifted his head up towards Vicki who sat near the back of the room.

"Vicki, we spoke of relationships, good and bad. How we try to make the most of things but when it all seems too far gone, we tend to give up on the people who were at one time closest to us. You and Tom grew further apart yet, even with finding a new interest in Paul you really still had some love held back for your husband. I had to ask myself why you even bothered to wait until Andy had left the office that horrible day before you ventured out from the Atkin building next door.

You said you felt ill that day of the murder and wanted to go home - but that's not true because you rang someone to ask a favour. To meet you on your way somewhere, at a specific time, in order to hand over the key and code of Andy's in order that he could still let Tom back into the Atkins building as usual on time. But you were also awaiting an official document through the office fax machine at Atkins before you could leave. Therefore you allowed young Andy to get away to his job delivering those letters prior to his getting to the match hopefully on time. You weren't so sure of getting there at all yourself as you had other plans.

Thomas here pointed it all out to me. You see this little town still has some CCTV like any other and it has helped out a lot in this case. When you had eventually left Atkins', you handed over the key card then went to 'Wainrights Emporium' on the high street. It didn't open on match days but it did for you. The reason was that you had arranged something special for Tom. Something that made us aware you had no real ill feelings for him, certainly not wanting to kill him. You had an arranged meeting with a solicitor to sign away your half of the home and contents owned by both of you. That may end up in ownership to his elder brother now by virtue of his death.

That meeting was in the company of a Solicitor in the offices above Wainright's for that whole time just preceding the murder. Paul was playing in the game and I am sure he did not know of your plans to disinherit yourself.

"You're telling me" sounded out Paul.

The Inspector continued.

"We spoke with the Solicitors and they confirmed your meeting and that the eventual consultation had forms duly signed and dealt with very quickly. The solicitor then left with you to walk up the street towards the stadium as he also lived that way. He witnessed you had to stop, meeting a trusted friend from the council who had a hand down a drain fetching out that very same key that someone had dropped into it by mistake not moments earlier, not long after collecting it from you. What a calamity.
Odd - yet nothing but the truth, all confirmed by the individuals concerned whom I have spoken to, placing you out of the frame."

Dilley swung left to face Elaine…"Isn't that right, Elaine? "
He walked over to Elaine and continued.

"You met Vicki, so were out for work from the stadium booking office and in your rush back dropped the key into the gutter and from there it fell down the drain. Luckily for you Vicki had contacts once you told her of the dilemma.

Though you were out of range of CCTV, we knew you were able to leave the stadium and go back to the drain, looking for Andy - who you had hoped had picked up your message by then to meet him there. Obviously you were unaware at this time that the key had been retrieved before you even got there, all persons having already left the scene.

After some time went by, you gave up and decided to get back to the stadium because Andy had not appeared and you obviously felt relieved when you saw Vicki back at the stadium booking office to bring - NOT THE KEY ITSELF - but the good news that it had been found. Such was your worry that Tom may have found out you had given flight a few times that day rather than be at work, looking for the key after initially losing it?... "Seeing Vicki must have felt like heaven."
Running scared, it was a miracle that he actually missed you when he was crossing over himself to the Atkin office close by .....But that's by the by now. We are here, he's gone and who did enter the building, killed Tom and got- he or she thinks - away with it?

"Yes, Sir, that's right," replied Elaine. 'I found out later when she caught up with me back at the stadium that she also had as much trouble as me with getting a phone signal just when it mattered.

"When I lost the key and called Vicki she said that she was busy but would try and get it sorted and see that everyone was ok. I still worried about it even though Andy text me to meet him by Atkins' as he couldn't get back to the stadium in time – knowing by then I should have it because Vicki had told him so. He had to deliver a last letter he said that made him late, then wanted the key, reason I wanted to see him there to retrieve it from the drain if possible, so he could let Tom in. I was so stressed. Seems he got fed up with waiting and dashed into the stadium to try and find Tom himself...Like you say - I missed him and Vicki as well as Tom. And what with poor coverage on my phone and Andy not returning a text I sent him I felt a need to try and at least see if he was there... I had asked him to meet me near Atkin's, by the drain some 200 yards from the front entrance. I even looked in the shops which took some time, so ended up getting back after Vicki in the end." She recalled.

"Thank You, Mrs Thompson" came back the Inspector. Then turning to her colleague he added.

"Also, for your information Maureen regards the visual on someone being around the bins when you dealt with the broken entrance door. A search revealed some blood on the binned plexi-glass and some recording equipment but all were clean of any prints. The police sound department has listened to the tape, badly muffled with tinny interference on it. It took a while to analyse this but sometimes you can be listening far too hard for something, but more on that later perhaps."

Turning his back upon all an answer came back.

"Chris Whittaker and Neil Edwards as accomplice obviously did it as they aren't here!" shouted out Bradley, arms folded, sat twitching.

"No, not so, young man, But you yourself may have been accused of all this, what with your poor work record with Tom and, indeed, so much going against you on that fateful day. If it weren't for the fact you did buy a ticket and then took a trip out of town to Chandale then Coventry, soon after you had spoken with young Andy in the street, you'd be a suspect too.

You told Andy what you were going to do to Tom and that could have had you in the cells by now. WELL, you needn't had bothered. Someone else has beaten you to it, but who?"

Talk about murder! Paul was seething and looking daggers at Vicki. Just when he was sure she was happy to be leaving the place with him. He also assumed it would be with a few more noughts in the bank balance than she was actually going to have. What was she thinking of? He was doing so well, new woman, new possible career off into Sheffield, living close by in Nottingham and now this bombshell! The death of Tom could have secured a good fortune in insurance, surely. But - now - what would he know after finding out this loss of ownership on the property that both Tom and Vicki had jointly owned. He couldn't wait to get his hands on her and there might be another murder!

Sergeant Thomas then came forth with a few things that gave Andy some kind of alibi. This meant that not only was he with Bradley in the street who was bemoaning of Tom but the butchers could say he was there just prior to his run up over to the stadium looking for Tom. And that was just when Chris Whittaker stopped him in the stadium in his tracks for that moment running about the place. Andy said he had given up looking when he received a phone call from Tom and then went over to Atkins' to find the horrible scene. That's when he found the body. Tom had called re-dial on his mobile and it got Andy's number at the time Andy was in the stadium actually looking for Tom, so shot up to the building quickly.

Then members of the assembled crowd started throwing questions at the two detectives.

Coach Chris said "As I was in the game and handed over my key to Dave Hallam at Tom's request I had no chance of being part of all these shenanigans. So why are we all here listening to this?"

David Temple soon chipped in "Hang on a minute; we've already heard that the secretary took Andy's key and mine was taken by Tom. So, how the hell could I get into the building - even if I wanted to?"

Then he turned to Chris to answer him, "Were you on the bench all the time? What about during the intervals and the way you always do your speeches and wander off. My key was taken from me by Tom himself so why the heck would he want yours as well?"

The reply came, "Listen mate. I can only tell you what happened. Dave Hallam came and took it from me. You need to explain how a dead man can defend you on that one".

As the two continued to bicker between other people's muttering, the Inspector came back into the conversation.

The Inspector turned and pointed towards Dave Hallam and said "Guys, please let's be civil …..Mr. Hallam will tell us more"

Having unexpectedly been brought into the conversation, Dave Hallam began to explain.

"It's true, Tom asked me to go and get a key from someone, so as I was nearer to the benches, I went and asked the coach for his"

At this Chris looked over to David and smirked. It was like a game between the two now.

 Continuing Dave Hallam said "I took the key and wondered why I was allowed to do so. Tom is so possessive as regards these, I thought that I needed a code number or something but Chris said just give it to him. I guess Tom knew what it was or what to do. I got to the corridor level again, just at that moment I saw Tom talking to David at the door of the equipment room and he was given another key card by David. It was similar to this one that I had and I figured I had been sent on a wild goose chase. So I was passing the changing rooms and decided to put the one I had into my own locker because Tom left the building. We all have a locker each for our clothes and things"

David Temple looked back over to Chris and smiled with the biggest grin of the day. "A ha, you see, not as smart as you think, boyo!"

"More likely Dave used the key himself to trip over to Atkins', following the manager" added Chris.

"No need looking for answers to that one "said Dilley. " I have those. You see, the key was still in the locker at the time of the murder. The club owner and the media people were making their way to the function room at the end of the second period and far too many witnesses saw David going into that locker to retrieve it again but at the same time a fractious Mark Atkin was scolding Mr. Hallam for wasting his time and so the key was put back as everyone moved on to answer a few questions in the function room and that lasted near all interval. David's key was found on the body of Tom…… 'Were any of the cards planted there' I hear you ask?"

"I don't hear anyone bloody asking" came the sudden reply from David.

"No, it wasn't planted" was a more acceptable reply for David's ears as the Inspector diverted everyone's attention to another topic, but not before another intervention.

"I thought Tom was found to have two key codes on him" asked coach Chris.

"Yes, one he had borrowed from Mr. Temple and the one given to him by Vicki which had originally been Andy's. She met Tom coming over from the stadium having just been given it by the council worker. Vicki's fingerprints were all over the key after the drain had cleared all previous marks, cleaned off also by the very good friend from the council who Vicki knew. The solicitor confirms he did not know anyone in the vicinity there when the key was handed over but that this had happened. The second key - as luck would have it for the equipment manager - was full of finger prints due to it being David 's and fresh ones which were Tom's."

If it were a birds eye view in evidence we'd see Vicki had bumped into Tom and handed him the key. She then moved on up the road to enter via the main gates to the stadium and Elaine thus missed seeing her, didn't find Andy, panicked and returned.

"Anyway, people. The reason why neither Chris Whittaker nor player Neil Edwards is with us is because they have both been arrested on separate charges. They could have been involved in this horrible business but, on this occasion, they were caught out in a separate crime - involving drugs. Their problem was that they brought it back here into their place of work. Great idea to gain more custom but it still threw open the chance of being seen with so many people about. However, it was not seen by the naked eye as such, the fine work of Chris Fielding got some nice snaps that we could look at. Enhanced photos taken from the mezzanine found both Neil and Chris down one of the exits in the stadium in the action of selling/buying the substance. This being around the time of the murder has helped exonerate them but indeed incriminated both for the handling/selling or buying of the unlawful class of drugs. Neil knew he was in trouble and confessed immediately, no wonder his game was in tatters of recent, Chris had nothing else to say once Neil helped us with our investigations. Chris admitted everything too.

"No wonder I could not find him" said Dave Hallam.

"Yes, He was in bits, annoyed with the injury and head full of mental turmoil but knew where to find Chris to be able to get a fix. He had plenty of interesting things to tell me when I met up with him, something also that had me scouring those CCTV cameras again. Whilst trying to keep a low profile and hiding behind a pillar in the corridor he heard the main door smash but was unaware of who the faces were who ran into the building through an originally locked door. It's understood that the assumed open entrances had been automatically locked and Neil brought the door situation to our thoughts once again when Maureen highlighted a lock down of doors. Reason why someone could not get in and had to bust the door open."

Dilley paced around the room to another part of it, where two people knew he was coming over to them.

He continued "It has been known for some time now that it is not just the bad running of the club that is of fault for its grave financial problem. I pursued Tom's own concern on this and in his M. A. Enterprises office found some notes of interest from a locked drawer, making accusation against his own staff. He needed to prove that club property was going missing and Geraldine, you were on the brink of being sacked. Along with Drew Blatherwick you had a scheme between you both to lighten the club of some more wares that could be sold on either a market or through friends.

How long did you two think that you could go on with this? Eventually people get caught out and as with our friends who embraced the illegal substance you also took something, less expensive but it all amounts to the same thing….criminal actions which are an offence to be dealt with. You and others (he looked over at Paul) are not out of the woods, we will be talking to some of you again."

Speaking back to all once again…..

"On this night Drew and his accomplice slipped out of the exit doors not realising that the manager had locked them when they were in the middle of off-loading merchandise to friends waiting outside. It must have come to some surprise that they could not get back in, locked out of the building, and not able to get back to chores cleaning that new boot room or on the mezzanine working the lights, yet would have some large excuse I'd imagine on your return. Geraldine, you even forgot about your meeting that you should have had at the end of the second period with Tom, lucky for you that you did. Crikey, you'd be up for more grilling on a murder charge if you had actually been over there at Atkins too'."

"When on the road off-loading their haul, Geraldine and Drew showed up on the CCTV as black figures in the distance just doing something seemingly quite normal. Then they were seen to be running back to one of the entrances."

"Out of the camera's view you tried the door yet could not get in. You got desperate I imagine, and then broke open the entrance which startled Neil on his way off from the ice surface. He stood back in the dark and you two probably thought you had gotten away with it. Drew caught his hand upon the glass on the way in but, with our forensic samples, we can eliminate both of you, knowing you had nothing to do with the murder. Unless you'd like to say you were at the crime scene after all…? It's a pity that a murder ensued and got in the way of your little scam. Furthermore, blood from Drew on that entrance door smeared onto Andy when he rushed back into the stadium."
So we have not one, not two, but three instances of misbehaviour- whatever their level that afternoon."

Drew chipped in:" I didn't worry too much and told Chris Fielding that I cared not of what Tom thought about me going missing - as I am about to retire and as I said to him Tom would have trouble sacking me because I was handing my notice in. But hell, I'd never kill the guy".

He then lifted his sleeve to show a wound from the action of breaking into the stadium, as if to admit them being at fault.

This gave the coach an opportunity to drop his bombshell that he'd been on the phone that game day also to another team and finalised a move to coach Aspley, "so I'm off also. I made a phone call to seal the deal and seem to have agreed a good contract. Sorry folks"

Dilley finalised…"Too late for all that Andrew, your retirement might not be in the place you'd hope for just yet. You and Geraldine will have to answer for your actions. However Chris you may be the only one here not to worry of what I am to say next."

Dilley knew he was nearer to explaining who the murderer was and what bad news everyone was in store for. For this he stood tall and was truly sorry to say:

"Grim news I am afraid for near all of you. From the effects of poor management, clear outrageous actions by those I have mentioned and just pure bad luck, it transpires that the company, 'Mustangs' in name, have gone bust. The owner has taken flight and when we caught up with him he told us that things had gotten a little difficult far earlier than he had expected. The team is thus disbanded as of now and the club does not exist anymore. I am sorry everyone but you are all now unemployed. "

There were a few gasps between murmurs and faces looked shocked, if it were possible after what had gone before. Lost jobs and - for Merrivale - it was an end to the local team that had struggled for so long. The good news of the great result against the Scorpions was not going to be followed up by further good times. There was not to be another game in the old blue building.

"I'm sorry to have had to tell you this but that's just how the cookie crumbles sometimes. My time here is now over too."

Inspector Dilley turned to face one in the crowd. The other police officers moved in to anticipate a possible bad reaction when the inspector leant over to David Temple and said:

'Which finally leaves me to say…………David Temple, you do not have to say anything. But it may harm your defence if you do not mention when questioned something which you later rely on in court. Anything you do say may be given in evidence."

Straight away the Inspector explained that David had left the stadium in order to commit premeditated murder and that he'd be interviewing him on those grounds back at the police station. Temple made complaints that turned to pleas, but the talking was all over. Only Vicki's gasps could be heard.

"You faked your being in the equipment room, it's your tape recording that we found in the bins and evidence galore all over it".

Two police constables came up behind Temple and stood waiting to link arms with him and take him away to the station. He was to be put in the cells until further notice of going to court and having justice prevail.

"If you will, please, Mr Temple, my colleagues would like to accompany you to an awaiting car outside and we'll meet again at the police station some time later."

Rather more lifted by the two constables then David raising himself, they took the long walk out of the building and down to the car. Everyone in the function room was left quiet whether it be from relief or shock, it didn't matter. All that remained was for them to disperse under the knowledge that they all had lost their jobs and were unemployed as of now.

Dilley and Thomas shook hands, Thomas turned to leave and Dilley placed his hand on the back and shoulder of Thomas as if to celebrate the accomplishment of what they had set out to achieve. The clearing up duties was to be left to the remaining police officers on site. All they need do now was interview Temple.

Vicki took time to contemplate and figure out what her next steps were. Cleared of any guilt, she took a moment by the bridge where Tom had proposed to her. She was now deliberating whether she should go to Sheffield at all. But she was not going to stay here in Merrivale for much longer.

The League table and division two as it stood

	Team	Pld	W (h+a)	D (h+a)	L (h+a)	GF	GA	Diff.	Points
1	Bramcote	17	11 (5/6)	5 (2/3)	1 (1/0)	74	48	+26	38
2	West Bridgeford	17	11 (5/6)	3 (2/1)	3 (1/2)	62	28	+34	36
3	Gedling	17	10 (7/3)	2 (0/2)	5 (2/3)	66	38	+28	32
4	Beeston	17	7 (4/3)	8 (4/4)	2 (1/1)	56	28	+28	29
5	Bulcote	17	8 (4/4)	5 (3/2)	4 (1/3)	44	28	+16	29
6	Eastwood	17	9 (4/5)	2 (1/1)	6 (4/2)	46	32	+14	29
7	Bestwood	17	8 (4/4)	4 (2/2)	5 (3/2)	42	32	+10	28
8	Wollaton	17	6 (2/4)	7 (4/3)	4 (2/2)	50	42	+08	25
9	Hucknall	17	6 (3/3)	6 (3/3)	5 (2/3)	40	44	-04	24
10	Toton	17	5 (3/2)	8 (3/5)	4 (3/1)	62	48	+14	23
**	*************								
11	Mapperley	17	6 (3/3)	5 (1/4)	6 (4/2)	28	32	-04	23
12	Carlton	17	5 (3/2)	6 (2/4)	6 (4/2)	42	42	00	21
13	Sherwood	17	5 (2/3)	5 (2/3)	7 (5/2)	34	46	-12	20
14	Clifton	17	5 (2/3)	4 (3/1)	8 (3/5)	44	64	-20	19
15	Bulwell	17	5 (4/1)	3 (1/2)	9 (4/5)	42	53	-11	18
16	**Merrivale**	**17**	**4 (2/2)**	**5 (3/2)**	**8 (3/5)**	**40**	**58**	**-18**	**17**
**	*************								
17	Aspley	17	4 (2/2)	5 (4/1)	8 (3/5)	38	64	-26	17
18	Colwick	17	3 (2/1)	6 (4/2)	8 (3/5)	30	48	-18	15
19	Lenton	17	3 (2/1)	3 (2/1)	11 (4/7)	36	66	-30	12
20	Meadows	17	1 (0/1)	4 (2/2)	12 (6/6)	28	62	-34	07

	Team	Pld	W	D	L	GF	GA	Diff.	Points
1	Bilborough	20	13	3	04	51	27	+24	42
2	Netherfield	20	11	7	02	56	38	+18	40
3	Forest Fields	20	12	3	05	59	32	+27	39
4	Radford	20	09	9	02	51	24	+27	36
**	**********								
5	St.Anns	20	09	6	05	36	26	+10	33
6	Dunkirk	20	08	8	04	45	35	+10	32
7	Sneinton	20	09	4	07	35	29	+07	31
8	Nuthall	20	08	6	06	33	36	-03	30
9	The Park	20	08	5	07	38	33	+05	29
10	Strelley	20	08	5	07	32	32	00	29
11	Highfields	20	06	9	05	54	49	+05	27
12	Highbury	20	07	5	08	30	38	-08	26
13	Cinderhill	20	06	6	08	39	36	+03	24
14	Basford	20	06	5	09	39	44	-05	23
15	Rise Park	20	06	5	09	35	48	-13	23
16	Stapleford	20	05	6	09	33	51	-18	21
17	Sandiacre	20	04	7	09	26	39	-13	19
18	Kimberly	20	04	5	11	29	53	-24	17
19	Brinsley	20	04	3	13	33	59	-26	15
20	Underwood	20	01	5	14	24	56	-32	08

Scene Sixteen Peoples Plight

A room of only four had the two investigating officers seated opposite David. At the door by which they had come in a sole policeman was guarding the entrance.

"Hey, no – come on. I didn't have a key card to get in." protested David.

"Why me?, I am one of several people who could have done it and admit that I told Dave Hallam the first aid key was over at Atkins' in a coat to delay him. I had to get it back from Wayne. How does any of this prove I am at fault? Blimey! Yes, I cut my hand on the skate sharpener and had to sort that but otherwise I was stuck in there all match - apart from taking a parcel back earlier on. Came out and spoke with Drew and Geraldine at that time. Even Dave Hallam came to ask about the first aid room key and saw me in there as you know as well as see Tom talking to me before he went with the loot to the safe."

Dilley closed his eyes. Then took a sharp in take of breath, as he was about to take over the conversation.

Dilley put his hand up with palm facing David as if to say 'stop'.

"You need me to explain. I and Thomas here have been through a few things, back at Atkin's. The building has a camera that operates on motion when people go into the coaching room where the safe is. The dating system on the photography had been deleted. But that didn't matter as it had been used correctly the evening prior. We'd not know what time of day it was that people went in or out of the room, but we do know for sure, that somebody with no interest in the safe was there just to meet up with Higson. Whether this was just a machine malfunction or someone's meddling hands, the vital pictures taken still tells us the story."

Dilley continued after taking another long breath.

"During the afternoon match you were in the equipment room for sure. You may have taken time earlier to visit the Atkins building to leave a parcel but you made sure people knew when you were supposed to be going and that you were seen to be back at the stadium later, telling people what you had done. You made sure that they believed you to be in the equipment room and working hard when you'd actually be out of the stadium committing the crime yourself. Yet if anyone saw you going over there, collecting the first aid room key from a left over coat was your ready made excuse and cover. The first aid key had always been with Wayne so all you had to do really was ask for it back.

You knew people would be less interested in how many skates had been sharpened that day with news of a murder under their noses. All that time spent in the equipment room but for such a small return of work and, of course, we know why now.

The tape recording we found in the bins outside was not of distortion as first thought but an actual recording of skate sharpening to make it appear that you were still in the room doing your job'. It had been damaged a little, of course, as you tried to destroy it and this fooled us a little but it clearly was a recording - without any interruption from the door being knocked upon by first Dave then Tom, should it have been a real live recording, which it wasn't. It was actually a recording on a loop - set by you to play when you were to leave the room disguised no doubt, hiding in the corridor from whoever might have been around at the time.

Setting the recording and leaving the room, you'd locked the door behind you. I guess being able to leave and return among the confusion of the front door being broken helped around that time too. So after taking a route clear of most CCTV cameras you followed the manager who had just taken the key card from you to get over to the Akin office to bank the takings as usual.

There was a short pause before the explanation continued.

No one was going to interject at this moment. It was all being taken in and consumed.

Letting the manager go inside you are aware that there is a 10 second delay before the closing door activates its lock. You managed to prevent this from happening by turning the handle - stopping this function - and you quietly opened the door yourself as Tom moved on upstairs. You sneaked inside and followed Tom up to the top level then to the room at the end of the corridor. He had just put the takings away when he turned to see you. Having made sure that you entered the room fully and away from any camera view which might have caught any scuffle, you attacked him. Sensibly near the back of the room out of sight but you'd not imagine someone a block away in the Chambers buildings of course watching all this happen.

What may have been said is unsure but someone from the logistics building opposite could just about see that an implement had been taken from a shelf and a fatal hit was given by a raised arm. Tom fell to the floor from just one blow. You then left and did not worry about the camera, because you'd be expected to have called upon the coaching room - of course - with a package earlier and duly the camera took an un-timed shot of you without a package as you left. It wasn't actually dropped off earlier, though, either was it? You had already placed it outside under the bushes on your first trip when you had spoken to Andrew and Geraldine saying you were doing just that. Obviously you'd not want two pictures of you going in that day so you left it to collect later. The package was still wet from being left in the soil outside and some of the parcel's cardboard had torn off as you retrieved it. My team searched the area and did a very good job – I love those guys. This was a cover story to make people aware that this was when you were taking the package over but if anyone happened to have seen you, you'd have to call off your mischievous plan I guess.

Given that Tom had taken your key you had to work quickly, retrieve the parcel and get in struggling with it if you were to keep up with him and grab that door before it locked behind him. The camera caught you with the parcel going in and without it going out, brilliant.

Tom was in a bad way but was still able to gather the energy to push the 'last number dialled' button on his phone and that was when Andy at the stadium got a call asking for help. Although Andy was unsure what was being said he knew it had come from Tom's phone saying, "I'm at Atkins, help me."

You made your exit with no time to close the door, indeed you wanted it to look as if someone had broken in, damaging the door a little as you passed. Then on your return, leaving the building quickly put the recording equipment into the bins, discarding it, as you thought, damaged enough to avoid recognition. Yet your own blood type from a wound had dripped onto this and glass in the bin proving your time was spent there. Maybe you had also been around the bins when Maureen had believed she saw someone as she was at the broken main entrance door.

Keeping apparently calm, David replied:

"No real proof that it was me - no prints; somebody else could have done all this."

These four gentlemen were the last people in the building.
The interview was coming to an end.
All that Dilley and Thomas had to do was come up with evidence that would convict in court.
Thomas sat back and awaited the final comments from his boss, something that they both had felt confident with.
Would this be enough to put Temple behind bars?

"The pictures taken by the camera - which we knew were only from that day - on exit/entry to the coaching room have proven you as guilty, David. You probably didn't know that the view from the camera clearly shows the three club awards on the shelf through the doorway. On all of the pictures that we have showing all the people going in and out, there are always three trophies standing on the shelf - even when you entered the room having taken off any disguise once you had got into the building carrying the parcel. But after attacking Tom with the fatal blow to the head with one of the trophies from the shelf you left the room with the weapon hidden to discard later. So your safety net of showing that you had been there supposedly earlier carrying a package into the room was good but the picture taken shows <u>only two</u> trophies on the shelf on you're leaving. If you had put it back on the shelf before leaving we'd possibly still be working on this case today."

David had no answer to this. He felt lost as to what to say. Caught out by these facts, his shoulders slumped and his head lowered as if to show he had given up in the fight to defend himself.

He was led away, faced court and was sentenced accordingly.

****

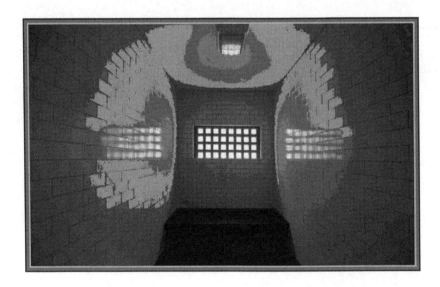

After the dust had settled.........

Paul was arrested on a charge of drugs possession. Leads had given the police enough evidence - along with the confession from security man Chris Whittaker owning up to dealing with the supply of drugs.
It was due to a dispute about another user who had not paid up for previous drugs that had him and Paul conspiring at the boards, claiming to want to 'Kill someone' for not paying up. Would there, in fact, have been a double murder this last weekend? The 'killing' they had previously mentioned at the pub prior to the match was in fact a good deal they had arranged regarding their drug dealings.

The wit of Bradley said it all:

"Could have sharpened some ice to a point, used this as a weapon, let it melt. He'd have gotten away with it then." .....Bradley never left Merrivale but took up a job at the construction works.

Tony Grainger, in fact, made tracks wanting to be rid himself of the whole situation and old enemy Chris so moved on to Chandale in search of job opportunities.

Chris Phillips took up that coaching job with Aspley. Antoine Marie-Jean, Dave Hallam and Chris Fielding struggled to find work. Elaine Thompson didn't need to and took retirement instead.

Both Sandi Stephenson and Maureen Smyth had some patching up to do with their respective husbands as players Barton, Collins, Edwards (stained with substance abuse record) Marshall and Pitchfork eventually managed to pick up places in other teams eventually.

Paul Hacking and Chris Whittaker both had gaol sentences fixed for their foreseeable futures but Andrew Blatherwick and Geraldine Ellis accepted community service orders.

DJ Dave England surprisingly came off the best. He played on at some venues with his jockeying skills then he bought a lottery ticket one day and won half a million and took the first train out of town.

Inspector Iain Dilley and Sergeant Neil Thomas stayed on at the police force for many a year till retirement and in Neil's case promotion came first which took him to Port Raven.

Andy Gill? Well he beat about the bush and kept to himself before making friends with new mates and lived a happier life outside of hockey.

Melanei, Ligaya, Richard and Jona all slipped into general life and made no further efforts to keep up with the sport. After all, Merrivale was now a ghost town as regards ice hockey.

Vicki moved to Derby and met a new man in her life.

Mark Atkin was never seen nor heard of again. But he was, for sure, alive and well and prosperous.

The murder weapon!
Was never found, it had been slung up onto the roof of a power station behind the stadium when chance allowed.

Was picked up by some interested magpie flying by but was dropped again into the murky woods of Morgantown. Not to be found again.

I think this is where they say. THE END

Thanks for your purchase.

THE **ICE HOCKEY** ANNUAL

Edited by Stewart Roberts

'The bible' of British ice hockey since 1976

Buy the latest edition in your rink
or at
www.icehockeyannual.co.uk

Elite League – EPIHL – NIHL – World Championships – and much more

****

Join the Supporters Trust

An organisation recently voted in to be the voice of the Nottingham Panthers fans.

Find out more by checking out the website...
www.pantherstrust.co.uk
facebook
@NottinghamPanthersSupportersTrust
or twitter @NPSupporters